THE GHOST'S DAUGHTER

THE GHOST'S DAUGHTER

THE ARMY BRAT HAUNTINGS
BOOK ONE

CARY HERWIG

*First, for my husband, who always encourages me.
Second, for all of the teachers in all the schools, in all the places we lived, from whom I learned so much.*

CHAPTER
ONE

June 1956, Camp Breckinridge, Kentucky

The door closed with a click. Vivien tried to turn the knob. The door had locked behind her. Now, they would have to find another way out.

"Sorry," Per said. "I thought it was unlocked when you opened it."

"I don't know. The door stood open."

She released the doorknob and her little sister, Lauren, tried to turn it. Vivien's heart pounded with the fear they might not be able to get out. They always did, every time they entered the old buildings. Fear of getting caught was part of the thrill. She took a deep breath and let it out slowly, the trick she'd learned to help when she became stressed.

"We should have tried it from the outside," Karl, Per's younger brother, said.

She rolled her eyes. Of course, they should have tried it. Why didn't they *think* before they let it close?

Their parents forbade them to be in the old hospital buildings. She and Per were both eleven and supposed to know better. But they couldn't resist. Until the pool opened for the summer, they had little to do. That wouldn't happen until more "summer soldiers" arrived for annual training. Until then, there weren't many people in the park. For now, the four of them had the old hospital for amusement, as long as they didn't get caught.

"Which way?" Vivien asked.

They knew of other unlocked doors. They'd found several before, so she knew they could get out eventually.

"That way." Per pointed down the hall. "It'll take us closer to home, and we know there are open doors."

She nodded. Before Vivien and her family arrived at Camp Breckinridge, the two boys had sometimes gone against their parents' orders not to go inside the old hospital buildings. As Army brats, they all knew their parents considered it important they obey orders, but curiosity always got the better of them. Now, Vivien couldn't resist the abandoned buildings. The mystery of them drew her. Some sort of treasure must have been left behind when the old hospital shut down. They only had to look for it. Whenever the others were reluctant to go inside, she talked them into going by telling them she would never tell what she found if she went alone.

Today they had entered by a different door than usual. Unlocked and open a crack, it proved to be irresistible. They'd identified several unlocked entries, but they liked to see if there were more. They memorized each location, sometimes using one previously discovered when they couldn't find a new one, especially when time for lunch. Once inside, it became a game as they searched for treasure and hoped to find an exit farther along.

There were four rows of the old buildings, sitting end to

end like railroad cars. Each building had four rooms. They were connected by narrow, enclosed hallways with windows on each side. Each building rested on concrete blocks.

The buildings at the end, farthest from the trailer park, connected to another of the enclosed hallways. A narrow road ran between, with two rows of buildings on each side. The main building, with one huge room on the ground floor, sat at the opposite end nearest the trailer park. The Moodys stored furniture and boxes in there, leaving a large empty space where they roller skated sometimes.

They had left home later than usual today. "Daddy will be home for lunch soon," Vivien said. "We need to get home or we'll be in trouble."

The sun shining in through the windows along both sides of the buildings made the enclosed space hot. The main road from headquarters to the trailer park ran along the side where the steps and doors were. On the other side, an empty, rectangular space overgrown with weeds separated the wood frame buildings.

They moved from room to room, trying to walk softly to keep the floors from creaking. They scanned floors and corners to see if anything interesting had been left behind. Although they spent many hours in the buildings, they never found anything more than dead birds and dry leaves lying on the dusty red linoleum floor.

None of them wore a watch, and Per and Vivien kept a lookout for either of their dads' car through the dusty windows while they moved down the corridor between buildings. Vivien checked the next entry door. They moved along the corridor between buildings and checked the next entry door. The rattle of the building as they walked reminded them of the trailers they lived in.

Once inside, they could go left or right. They never found

any door opening toward the other row of buildings unlocked. If they wanted to get into those, they would have to go outside and around to the next road. They went over there only once, and not one door gave them entry. They decided it was too dangerous anyway, because they couldn't see when one of their fathers drove by from there.

They tested another door but found it locked and they couldn't escape through that one. "We've walked miles," Lauren said, her usually sweet voice now a whine.

Most times they didn't get too far from an escape route. Except today, when the door they got in locked behind them. They had no exact idea where the next open door might be.

They were testing the third door when Per whispered, "There's your dad,"

They all crouched below the windows so he wouldn't see them.

"We gotta find an open door," Lauren said, "or we'll be in trouble."

They stood as one and Vivien looked out in time to see the white Chevy disappear to the left. With a start, she saw her reflection in the glass, knowing in an instant it didn't look like her. When she blinked the image faded. The others had moved on. She glanced around. She was alone.

She caught up with the others hurrying along the corridor, hoping the next outer door would be open. The second one opened and, first looking up and down the road, they piled down the wooden steps. They ran for a while but slowed to a fast walk as the noontime heat got to them.

When they reached the trailer park, they separated, heading for their own homes. "See you after lunch," they called to each other.

The sisters stopped outside of the trailer to catch their breath before going inside. Daddy sat at the table, eating his tuna salad sandwich. Mama smiled when they came in and told them to wash up. Usually, when she smiled like that, it meant Daddy was in a good mood.

As he ate, he read the newspaper he brought home. When he went back to work, he always left it. Vivien usually picked it up and read as much as she could. Not all of it made sense to her, but what she did understand told her much about the world.

She pushed ahead of Lauren and got to the sink in the bathroom toward the back of the trailer. Quickly, she washed and dried her hands, blocking her sister from reaching the sink. Lauren tried to get around her, then stood back, leaning against the hall wall.

Finished, Vivien brushed past her sister, heading for the kitchen. Sandwiches sat on the every-day plastic plates on the small table. Bought used, they'd lived in this trailer for nearly a year. It measured ten feet wide by fifty feet long, large when compared to their earlier one, which was only eight feet by thirty feet. House trailers, more and more often called mobile homes, included all of the usual furniture, fixtures, and appliances, with lots of overhead storage.

The master bedroom took up the back, separated from the hall by an accordion door. The girls' bedrooms, between the kitchen and bathroom, had no privacy. Their beds took up one side of the hall and built-in dressers and closets took up the other side. Although they were open to the hall, having their own space was so much better than sharing a fold-out sofa in the living room.

Mama sat down once the girls were at the table. They ate in silence for a while. Conversation didn't start until Daddy finished eating. He folded the first section of the newspaper beside his plate.

"Another hot day," he said. Everyone nodded. "You girls been playing with the Moody boys, today?"

"Yes, Daddy," Vivien said.

They finished the sandwiches and cold glasses of sweet iced tea in silence. Daddy picked up the other section of the newspaper, folding it on top of the first when he'd finished.

"You girls be careful where you play," he said as he got up.

Mama stopped clearing the table and gave him a kiss before he stepped out the door. The whole trailer vibrated, just like the hospital buildings, when he stepped down on the metal steps that folded out from under the door.

"Bye, Daddy," the girls called out as the aluminum screen door clicked shut. He waved as he crossed the concrete slab that served as both porch and patio.

After the Chevy turned the corner, they asked Mama if they could go on over to the Moodys' and play canasta.

"Give them a break for a bit," she said. "You can go over in half an hour or so."

The Moodys' trailer sat against a sort of sunroom built permanently on that site. Mr. Moody, a Chief Warrant Officer, managed the campground. In less than a month, summer soldiers would arrive, mostly in the Reserves and National Guard. Camp Breckinridge had been built during the Second World War, including the hospital complex. During the war, thousands of German prisoners were held there. During the Korean War, the Army used it for infantry training. Now, it operated as a training post in the summer for part-time, civilian soldiers. Wilderness surrounded the post, with wild blackberries growing with abandon. Fruit trees grew in unlikely places.

The Army sent Daddy there just for this summer to help with the training. Where they would go in the fall they couldn't guess, but it would be overseas. The Moodys would stay until next year. Daddy had been transferred there from Fort Knox before the school term ended. They pulled their trailer into the park in May. Teachers in a military town knew about these sudden moves, and they had given the girls passing final grades, even though they lacked a week of finishing the term. Such things happened in the life of Army brats.

Vivien sat on the picnic table on the concrete slab they used for a patio, with her feet on the bench. A breeze ruffled the pages of the newspaper as she tried to read it. One article reported on China and Korea. Daddy served in Korea during "the war" and she tried to understand the story but found it hard to concentrate.

Her stomach hurt, it was hot, and she wanted another glass of iced tea. She started to jump down when Mama came out the back door of the trailer. She held a pair of Vivien's underpants, the ones she'd hidden in the dirty clothes hamper that morning because they were soiled.

So, Mama found them and now there would be a lecture. Vivien sat back down, and Mama sat beside her. Lauren looked up from her book on the other side of the table.

"Remember when I told you about your becoming a woman some day?"

Vivien nodded. Mama held up the panties.

"The time has come," she said. "You've started your first period."

Vivien searched her memory for the earlier conversation. She remembered Mama telling her what would happen, that it meant she had become a woman when it did. Mama also said it was a necessary part of becoming a mother someday.

She remembered being horrified at the prospect. What if she didn't want children? What if she never got married?

Her stomach still hurt. "Menstrual cramps," Mama said.

"Will it always hurt like this?"

"No," Mama said. Vivien suspected her mother had her fingers crossed behind her back.

TWO

The dime store had everything they needed. Vivien climbed into the back of Mrs. Warner's Buick, clutching the brown paper bag.

Mama had told Mrs. Warner what happened and asked if she would take them into town to get the necessary items. As she drove, the older woman told Vivien how wonderful to be grown up now.

Vivien didn't feel more grown up. Mostly she felt confused and embarrassed.

When they got home, Mama showed how the sanitary belt worked with the Kotex pad. The bulk felt awful between her legs. The only question she asked was, "How long do I have to wear it?"

"It's hard to tell at first," Mama said. "When you get regular, it will probably be for four or five days. Right now . . . well, we'll just have to wait and see." She repeated how special a moment it was in a girl's life since it made it possible for her to have her own children one day. At that moment, Vivien would gladly give up that whole blessing forever.

Mama also told her that this meant she could no longer play like the boys did. When she asked why, Mama didn't answer the question.

"Sometimes I worry about you," Mama said. "You're so independent and smart."

"Is that bad?"

"Maybe. Most men don't like independent women or smart women. When a woman is both . . ." She shrugged.

"You're smart," Vivien said.

Mama smiled. "But your father doesn't know it."

Vivien thought about how her father treated her mother. He often asked her what she thought they should do when there was a choice to be made. Mama most of the time said, "Whatever you think." Every so often, though, she expressed an opinion. Sometimes, they did what she suggested. But not often.

When they left for the store, Lauren had gone over to the Moodys' to play cards with the boys. She asked what happened, why couldn't she go, too. Mama had put her off until they got home from the dime store. The little sister ran home when she saw them getting out of the car, immediately letting them know how unfair she didn't get to go, too.

"You're too young," Mama said. "One day, in a couple of years, you will become a woman, too." That explanation confused her since Mama hadn't set her down for "the talk" yet.

Vivien moped around, as the day dragged on. Her stomach hurt, and the pad chafed. She grabbed one of her books on natural history and went out to the picnic table to read. Shade covered it as the sun moved past zenith.

"Are you okay?"

She looked up and saw Lauren standing shyly in front of

her. She bit back a curt reply. *No, I'm not okay. No, I'm not happy. Yes, I want to die.*

But she held her tongue. "I'm all right," she said grudgingly.

Lauren sat beside her and swung her legs. "Is this going to happen to me, too?" Mama had already said it would, but she could see Vivien was unhappy.

"Yeah. In a few years."

"Do you want it?"

"No."

"Neither do I."

Lauren started reading the book she'd brought out. Vivien sat quietly, watching her sister out of the corner of her eye. She thought she loved her little sister, but much of the time, she found her irritating, always wanting to follow her around, bothering her when she read, breaking her things.

Today, mutual distrust of growing up bound them to each other, and what it meant to be a woman. It wasn't going to be as much fun as she had thought it would be.

"So, you've got a bloody nose."

Daddy's voice boomed out from the hallway as he walked through to the bathroom. Vivien continued washing her hands. Her face got hot, and she saw in the mirror that it looked bright red. She ignored him, looking past him at her mother. She'd betrayed her.

"Good for you," Daddy went on. "'Bout time you grew up."

She didn't want to sit at the table with everyone. They all knew now, and Daddy teased her. Lauren laughed as he did, wanting to be part of the joke that she didn't understand. Of course, Vivien didn't understand it, either.

Daddy tired of the teasing and started complaining to Mama about the Commanding Officer and what went on at headquarters. "The CO doesn't know his ass from a hole in the ground," he said, not for the first time.

Mama sympathized as always and cut her eyes at the girls, warning them not to repeat his language. None of them really understood what Daddy did or what HQ really meant. Although he complained a lot, he never really said much about the day-to-day goings on.

The girls cleared the table and started washing the dishes. The adults went outside to sit at the picnic table. A light breeze blew. Inside, the trailer felt hot as an oven. Daddy had promised to get a large fan more than a week ago, but it hadn't appeared. News came on the radio that Mama kept on all day. Vivien had gotten so that she didn't hear it much anymore. She figured Mama didn't either.

This time, the announcer began with the weather, describing the possibility of storms coming. The partly sunny sky contradicted the dire warning, so they felt safe from anything for a while. Kentucky sat within what everyone called tornado alley, with summer storms too often a problem.

Once the dishes were put away, Vivien asked Mama if she could go for a walk. Lauren wanted to come too, but she brushed her sister off. She wanted to be alone. The day had been exhausting and frustrating, and as she usually did when life got complicated, she wanted to be alone to think.

Mama checked her watch and said she could go. "Don't go very far. I want you home before dark."

With daylight savings time, it got dark late, now. Vivien promised to be back in time and started off.

She walked toward the hospital headquarters building, on a slight rise just beyond the edge of the trailer park. She turned and looked back. The trailer park lay very flat. Over fifty trailers could be parked there, but now only five sat in place. Three parked close to each other – hers, the Moodys', and the Warners'. They looked like they'd huddled together so they wouldn't be lonely.

The Warners were an old, childless couple, at least in their fifties, who had just come back to the States from Japan. Vivien visited them to hear their stories of Japan and look at the things they brought home with them. She hoped Daddy might be stationed there one of these days.

She turned left along the road bordering the park, then right, up the road that passed the derelict complex where the four of them usually went. The always found one of the nearest doors unlocked. When she wanted to be alone, she went there.

The hinges squealed when she opened the door, loud enough to wake the dead. The trailers sat far enough away that no one could hear it. Still, it grated on her ears, and again when she closed it. She turned to the left, through the corridor then into the next building. That door squealed, too, echoing through the emptiness.

The red linoleum, slickened by a thin layer of dust, made skating in the main building more fun. Slick enough to be dangerous, and Vivien found it exciting. After skating on such a smooth surface, she hoped to never have to skate on a concrete sidewalk again. Add a pair of shoe skates, instead of clamp-on skates, which always came loose and tripped her, would be perfect. Something else they couldn't afford.

They often used this entrance to get into the building for their explorations, coming out down the way. If she thought about it, they'd likely tried every door along this side. She didn't think anyone else came here alone. She backed up against the far wall and slid down it to the floor. Pulling her knees up to her chest, she wrapped her arms around her legs and put her chin on her knees. The air felt chilly, and she shivered. Curious. The sun still shone bright.

Silence filled the air. Dust she'd stirred up floated in the light from the window.

She sighed and closed her eyes. Growing up wasn't all it was cracked up to be. Hair appeared where it shouldn't be, now blood and cramps made her miserable, and she would have to suffer with all of it every month for the rest of her life. Mama tried so hard to make her believe the wonder of it, but she just couldn't.

"It happens to all women," a voice said.

Vivien's head jerked up and she looked side to side. No one else in the room. Maybe she had fallen asleep and dreamed that someone spoke.

She started to get up and leave. The voice, or illusion, broke the spell since she no longer felt alone, and the air had grown cooler, raising chill bumps on her bare arms and legs.

"You aren't alone," the voice spoke again.

THREE

Her heart pounded so loud she could hear it, feel it thumping against her ribs. Slowly, she pushed herself up with her legs, keeping her back against the wall. Someone wanted to scare her.

"Is that you, Lauren? I told you not to come."

Silence.

"Per? Karl?" She listened. "Who's there?"

She tried to swallow the lump in her throat. The door loomed on the opposite wall, and she would have to cross the room to get to it. Light from the setting sun and the few street-lights that had turned on showed nothing in her way, no one else in the room.

Should she run? Or move toward the door slowly?

A breeze ruffled her hair, stirring the dust on the floor. The hinges squealed when the door opened. Someone had to have opened it and they could be standing right outside. But she couldn't see anyone.

She called out again. "Hello?" and the breeze rose.

"Vivien," a voice called softly.

She bolted for the doorway, holding out her hands to keep it from closing on her. She ran to the outer door in the corridor, opened it to the outside, jumped from the top step, and ran.

The smooth surface of the road made running easy. In the gathering darkness, her long legs carried her along at a good pace. The trailers sat in the last glow of the day. She slowed. If her parents saw her running, they would think something happened.

Nothing wrong. No voices in the dark. Just a horrible day.

Mama and Daddy sat at the picnic table with the Moodys. Lauren and the boys played hide and seek. Per leaned against the trailer and counted to a hundred by tens. Vivien sat at the far end of the table from the adults, trying to hide her breathing hard. Mama turned and smiled at her, then went back to their conversation.

With a sigh, Vivien closed her eyes. *Everything okay. Safe. Nothing happened. Not really.*

They loved playing hide and seek in the dark. Darkness lay between the pools of light from streetlights and pole lights at some of the pads. Per found Lauren and she shrieked.

"Not so loud," Daddy called out.

She saw Vivien and came running. "Come on, Viv. We're playing hide and seek. You're late, so you're it next time."

Vivien huffed. As the big sister, she resented Lauren for always wanting to be around. She could often be impatient to the point of being mean. The rest of the time, she tried to ignore her. But no one else had better ever try to hurt her.

Should she as a young woman, be playing children's games? Just because she did most nights, didn't mean she should keep doing it. Mama said she couldn't play like a boy anymore.

She couldn't resist and jumped up when the new game started. Playing distracted from everything. Covering her eyes, she counted— "ten, twenty" — to a hundred. Lauren always hid in the same place, behind the Moodys' trash can. She found her, then Karl. Time ran out before she found Per, and they were all called in for bed.

They went from cooler air outside into warmer air in the trailer. As she washed up for bed, Vivien wished they could afford an air conditioner. Heck, they couldn't even afford a color TV. True, not many people had those either, but it would be nice. At least they often enjoyed the coolness in the Moodys' sunroom when they played canasta with the boys. And once they could go swimming, life would be better. But Mama said she couldn't swim when she had her period. That thought brought her mood back down.

She lay there, feeling sweaty and sticky, trying all the while not to remember the voice in the old hospital. She must have imagined it. What else could it be? A ghost?

There's no such thing as ghosts.

But why would she imagine a voice speaking to her? It might have been that scary movie, *Them*, she saw last weekend. She did sometimes have nightmares after she watched really scary movies. But she was awake when she heard the voice, and it had been several days since she saw the movie.

Everything that had happened the whole day scared her.

She sighed and stuck her feet out from under the sheet. The Kotex pad made her uncomfortable. Mama had helped her change it before she went to bed.

Not for the first time, she thought that growing up wouldn't be any fun at all.

Vivien studied her figure from the waist up in the mirror over the sink. She wished they had a full-length one. She was supposed to be a woman now, yet the shirt lay flat against her chest. She looked down at legs that still looked like sticks below the shorts. No woman's body here. Maybe it would begin changing soon.

Her dark mood matched the day with grey clouds hiding the sun. After breakfast, Mama told the girls not to go too far. It looked like there might be a storm, which this time of year might bring tornados.

The air, still and close, sapped her desire to do anything, much less play. Plus, her stomach still hurt, although not as bad as yesterday. The realization she bled off and on all day seemed too much to bear.

Lauren sat next to her, talking, trying to cheer up her big sister. Vivien ignored her.

"Why did Mama name us after movie stars?" Lauren asked after a short silence.

"What?"

"Why did Mama . . ."

"I don't know. She didn't like any of the family names – you know, Grandma and our aunts. She loves the movies. So, why not?"

"I don't know. Other kids tease me sometimes."

"About your name?"

"Yeah. When I tell them I'm named after Lauren Bacall."

"Don't tell them." Mama had named her after Vivien Leigh.

Her little sister looked down, hugging her knees. Vivien felt bad for yelling.

"Okay. If you don't like your name, we could come up with a nickname."

"Like what?"

For the next several minutes Viven suggested other names. "I read once in a movie magazine Lauren Bacall's friends call her 'Betty'."

"I don't like it much." Lauren though a minute. "I always liked 'Susie'."

"Too common. Lauren isn't common, you know."

"I guess."

Vivien kept hoping the boys would come out. Or she could get her book. Mama had signed a card for her to get books from the adult section of the library where they went once a week. They both usually grabbed several to last until the next week. She'd nearly finished *The Count of Monte Cristo*, her current book. She loved reading novels by Alexandre Dumas, even though he used a lot of words she didn't know. The heroes were so brave and romantic, and what girl wouldn't want to be the one loved by D'Artagnan or Edmond Dantes.

A clap of thunder announced the coming storm, followed by large drops of rain. They jumped down from the table.

"Come inside, girls," Mama called through the screen door.

Looked like a morning of reading, then. But Mama had other ideas.

"You two can help with the cleaning."

Vivien took charge of the vacuum cleaner, and Lauren did the dusting. Ever since her parents bought the Hoover Constellation she loved using it. Being round and small, it didn't take up much room. It floated above the floor on its exhaust air, which made it easy to pull behind her. She imagined it as an invention in one of the futuristic science fiction novels she loved to read.

Mama kept the radio on, listening for any weather warnings, even though the vacuum drowned it out along with the drumming of rain on the roof. One of the jalousie windows in the living room leaked a bit and they mopped up water every so often.

Just as she was finishing up the living room rug, the lights flickered and the vacuum cut off. Vivien looked up. A figure passed by the window. Who would be out in this downpour?

The lights stayed on and the vacuum roared into life. They soon had the trailer spick and span. Vivien finally lay on her bed reading when the rain stopped, and a knock came on the door. Mama called out, "It's Per wanting to know if you girls want to go outside."

"Yes," Vivien answered. She got up and walked through Lauren's bedroom. She lay on her back, sound asleep, her book lying on her chest.

"Where's Karl?" she asked as she stepped outside.

"He fell asleep while it rained."

"So did Lauren."

"Want to explore the hospital some more?"

They had walked in the direction of the line of old buildings. The day had turned muggy. Her shorts and shirt stuck to her skin.

She remembered the voice speaking to her when she went alone last night. She didn't really want to go back there, but if she was with Per, she wouldn't be alone this time. It would be safe.

They walked up the hospital road and talked about their siblings. What pests they could be. How great it felt to not have them following.

They located the open door they used most often, and the one she used the previous evening. Inside, she started to go in the opposite direction, but changed her mind. Hands balled into fists, she crossed the threshold. Maybe she could see what caused her to hear a voice.

"What is it?" Per asked.

"Nothing." She walked over to the wall where she sat before. The imprint from her butt showed in the dust. "I came here last night. I thought I heard someone's voice."

"Someone else was here?"

She shrugged, not wanting to talk about it.

"Maybe an escaped prisoner," he whispered. "What did they say?"

"Only one voice, a woman, and she called my name."

He looked at her a moment. "That's spooky."

"Yeah. A prisoner wouldn't know my name."

"Maybe someone's been hiding here for a while and they heard us calling to each other."

It made some sense. Except, if someone else hid in these buildings, it might not be safe for them to be here, even now. Maybe the woman didn't want people knowing she stayed here and scared them so they would leave.

"Could it have been a ghost?" Per asked "Lots of people could have died in here."

"There's no such thing as ghosts." She put as much disdain in the words as she could. But she'd had the same thought last night. Like skating on the dusty floor in the storage area, the possibility was exciting and scary at the same time.

Per asked what she was doing when she heard the voice. She told him she'd been sitting against the wall. They went to sit in the same spot, to see if the voice would speak again. After several minutes, they gave up.

"Maybe it only speaks to girls."

She started to tell him she wasn't a girl anymore, but she feared he'd ask how she knew. She didn't totally understand the explanation herself and he would make fun of her like Daddy did.

She would just have to come back alone and see what happened.

They went on to explore as usual. Too soon, they spotted her father's car and went back to the door they used when they came in. The air warmed up again after the storm, but it felt cool enough for them to run full tilt to get home in time for lunch. She opened the screen door and stepped up.

"Quite a rain we had," Daddy said.

Lauren sat at the table. Mama, as always, fussed around, while everyone else started eating — bologna sandwiches this time. Vivien preferred it fried, but cold with mayonnaise, a big slice of tomato, and lettuce tasted good, too.

"Looks like the pool will be opening next week," Daddy said.

"Really?" Lauren squealed.

He smiled at her. "That's the plan."

Finally. Vivien really wanted to learn to swim better, at least as well as Mama. They could use the pool for free, so she would learn this summer. And Mama promised her period would be over by then.

The temperature rose during the afternoon and the girls went to the Moodys to play cards. The air-conditioned room felt cool, almost heaven. But her preoccupation with the pool kept her from concentrating. She lost every game.

Soon they were called home for supper. After the kitchen had been cleaned up, they all sat at the picnic table drinking iced tea. The heat and humidity stayed high and the evening air remained sticky. A few mosquitos buzzed around them and a host of bugs closed in on the pole light beside their trailer. After a while, the Warners came to visit.

"It's too hot in the trailer," Mrs. Warner said. "At least there's a breeze out here."

Vivien got bored with the grownups' conversation. She thought about going back to the room in the hospital. She needed to know if the voice was real.

Lauren and the boys played hide and seek again. Their shouts followed Vivien as she walked back to the hospital. She needed to prove to herself no ghost haunted that building. Whatever spoke to her had to be either a person or her own imagination.

If no one spoke this time, then she imagined the voice before.

She reached the steps leading up to the door and stood looking at it. Squaring her shoulders, she went up the steps and opened the door. Darker inside, just like before, with only enough light to move around without tripping over something. She turned left, into the room. In the daylight, with Per by her side, the space hadn't been scary. Now, in the shadows cast by the lowering sun, it felt cold and threatening.

She went to the opposite wall and sat on the floor, just like before. She realized she'd planned to come back all day, without thinking about it. Something in her didn't like to be scared. She didn't like roller coasters or horror movies. Even when her father made her afraid, losing his temper, yelling and cursing, she rebelled, receiving a few swats in the process. Now, she sat quietly, searching the darker corners. The light dimmed outside the windows. She would face whatever it might be, telling herself not to be afraid.

"You came back."

The voice was as soft as before, non-threatening. Yet, it frightened her.

"Who are you?"

"Are you still unhappy? Still wishing you didn't have to grow up?"

"What do you want?"

"Nothing. Everything."

"That's no answer." Vivien pressed her back flat against the wall.

"I don't owe you an answer."

"Then quit bothering me."

A soft chuckle. "I couldn't bother you if you didn't come here alone."

"Or at night?"

Silence, as if the voice contemplated its answer. "Day or night is of no consequence."

"So, if I came here during the day, you would speak to me?" Silence. "If I came alone then, you would speak to me." Silence. "You like scaring little kids?"

"Are you scared?"

"A little. Maybe."

"You aren't a kid anymore. You are a woman, now."

Everyone said so, but Vivien didn't believe it. She didn't want it. Mama said she could now have children, thinking Vivien would be pleased. Of course, she wanted to do lots of grownup things. Right then, having children was not one of them.

"You will want them. One day," the voice said.

"You can read my mind?" Silence. "You guess, don't you?"

She stood and checked every corner. The quarter moon had risen in the twilight sky and gave a little light. It and the setting sun showed the grassy space between buildings. The road on the other side reflected light through the windows of the next building and the empty bridge between buildings. Where could the woman hide?

"I'm going home," she said, looking over the room once again. No visible hiding place inside, just a square box with windows on two sides. She'd heard the voice. A thrill of excitement ran through her. She asked out loud, "Are you a ghost?" She never believed in such things, but what else could it be?

"No."

"A spirit?" Was there a difference.

"I am lonely."

"Can you leave this building?" Silence. "I'm going home. I won't be back since you won't tell me anything."

The building rattled. Vivien struggled to keep her footing. For a moment, she thought, tornado, but the moon, higher in the sky, shone brighter now the sun had fully set.

"You will come back. I have need of you."

"If I don't?"

"I know where you live. And who lives there with you."

For an instant, Vivien stopped breathing. Her chest tightened. She rose up on shaky legs. "Don't you dare hurt my family."

INSTEAD OF RETURNING TO THE HOSPITAL THE NEXT DAY, THE FOUR OF them played cards and read. They wandered around the post, into areas they probably shouldn't be, making it more exciting. The rest of the week they spent at the pool with brooms and shovels to clean out the leaves and other debris. If they cleaned it out, maybe it would open sooner.

Keeping busy helped Vivien push the woman's voice to the back of her mind. When she thought of it, she told herself someone played a joke with her, trying to scare her. A mean thing to do and she couldn't think of anyone so mean.

Oh, Daddy could be pretty mean sometimes. When he got really mad, he hit Mama, but not very often. And always sorry afterward, just like when he hit her or Lauren. He hit them less often. He usually left disciplining the girls to Mama.

She remembered the time when their kitten took sick. Its eyes became infected. He took it outside to treat the poor thing with some sort of medicine, but the cat was frightened and bit him, and made him mad. He broke its neck.

She'd cried when she found out. For several days, she avoided him. Other times, she repeated to herself what Daddy said: the cat didn't hurt anymore.

When Daddy did those things, Mama always told them he was under a lot of stress. The Army wasn't an easy career. Much of the time, he showed her great affection. He was mostly tolerant of the girls. They knew he loved them, even if he didn't often express it. Since they'd come to Breckinridge, there hadn't been any outbursts.

But now, the job of getting the pool cleaned out, and the company of Per and Karl, even Lauren, chased most of the dark memories away. The best thing, her period stopped and she could swim in the pool when it opened.

SIX

Vivien counted the seconds between flashes and rumbles. Saturday evening, hot and humid, with clouds rolling across the sky, playing with lightning and thunder in the distance. No close lightning strikes, yet.

The music on the radio stopped frequently for the weatherman to give a report on conditions. When he warned of a possible tornado, they all perked up. They lived in a trailer, in a flat open area, without a shelter for miles.

"What about the hospital?" Vivien asked. It had to be safer than the trailer.

"It's higher than we are here," Daddy said. "Probably the first thing to be hit."

"Tornado on the ground two miles south of Breckinridge, moving toward the post." Why didn't the weatherman sound excited or scared?

Daddy herded them all outside and into the car. With the dark storm and the sun setting, the lightning flashes lit up the sky for mere seconds. Mama turned on the car radio as Daddy headed off post toward town.

They had just entered town when the weatherman announced the tornado disappeared. They turned around and returned home. Rain pounded the roof of the trailer for the rest of the night. Vivien went to bed but didn't think she'd be able to sleep. She woke once to hear the radio in the living room, the volume turned very low. Mama sat at the kitchen table until the storm had passed in early morning.

The air felt less muggy when the girls stepped outside Sunday morning. The Moodys were going into town to a movie, so there'd be no playing cards in the air conditioning. Being stuck at home made Vivien irritable until Daddy announced more families would arrive soon and post maintenance people had begun getting the pool ready.

By Sunday afternoon, Vivien got bored. Without something to keep her busy, her thoughts turned to the woman. She was strange, whoever she might be. Maybe what sounded like a threat to Vivien's family was only words. Whoever she was, Vivien felt both curious and afraid.

She picked up her new book — *Mysterious Island*, the follow-up to *20,000 Leagues Under the Sea*, by Jules Verne — but couldn't get into it. Her curiosity about the woman intruded. Too many questions without answers. Each time the voice spoke, Vivien felt darkness fold around her.

Because you were there in the dark, dummy.

But was that all? She had to go back. She told Mama she wanted to go for a walk. When Lauren heard, she begged to go, too.

"No, I just want to walk alone and think."

"Think about what?" Lauren demanded.

"Everything. Life."

Mama smiled. Vivien suspected her mother didn't think she knew much about life. She knew some things and wondered about other things. Alone.

"You've been reading too many of my books," Mama said. She belonged to the Book-of-the-Month Club and got many of the recent bestsellers. Vivien believed she learned so much about life in those and the books she checked out from the library.

"Take her with you," Mama said. "And don't go far."

"Aww . . ." Vivien started to stomp her foot, but remembered, according to Mama, only children threw tantrums, and she had become a young woman and she should act like one.

In spite of her best intentions, she stomped out of the trailer, jumping down to the concrete slab. She stalked off, not checking to see if Lauren kept up.

Why become a young woman if she still had her little sister tagging along?

"Slow down, Viv."

She walked faster, almost breaking into a run. She knew better, because if Mama saw her, there would be hell to pay.

Heaving a big sigh, she slowed down. Having Lauren with her could be a good thing. If the woman spoke with both of them there, at least there would be a witness. If she didn't, then it meant the voice would only speak to her. In a way, it made her feel special, but having someone with her gave a bit of comfort.

All of these musings ended as they reached the door into the hospital. Vivien walked up the steps and reached for the door.

"You're going in there alone?" Lauren said.

"No, you're with me."

"I mean, just the two of us?"

"Yes."

"But it'll be dark soon."

"It won't be dark for hours. There's nothing to be afraid of."

But not knowing if the voice was real made her unsure.

SEVEN

Taking a deep breath in the hot, sultry room, Vivien went to the same wall and sat on the floor. She leaned back and looked up at Lauren standing in the doorway, clearly uncomfortable about being there.

"You wanted to come," Vivien said.

"Yeah, but —"

"Come, sit."

Her little sister stayed in the doorway, looking down at the floor.

"It doesn't feel right."

"What doesn't?"

"Being here."

"We've been in here a hundred times."

"Hello, Vivien's sister."

The voice was low, friendly. Lauren's eyes widened and she looked about to bolt.

"What is that?"

Although Vivien had heard the voice before, her throat went dry. She swallowed before she said, "A voice."

"Yeah, but who is it?"

"I don't know." Vivien started to tease Lauren about being afraid but thought better of it. She stood and her sister moved to stand beside her.

"It's Per. Or Karl," Lauren said. "Trying to scare us."

A soft laugh filled the room.

"Is it a ghost?" Lauren whispered.

"Probably."

"Why is the hospital so quiet?" the voice asked. "Where are all of the doctors and nurses? The patients?"

"It's been closed for years," Vivien said. "Since the war ended."

"The war is over?"

Vivien nodded, not knowing if the ghost could see her, and said, "Yes."

"When?"

"A long time ago. Ten years, maybe."

"Such a long time?" The woman sounded surprised. "I've slept so long."

Lauren and Vivien looked at each other. Was the woman dead or waking from a long sleep?

"Can we see you?" Vivien asked. "It's spooky hearing your voice, but not seeing you."

A dim mist gathered, swirled, colors shimmering like a rainbow. It looked just like ghosts who appeared in movies. Did the people who made those movies know what real ghosts looked like?

A woman's form appeared in a nurse's uniform. Lauren edged closer to her sister and for once, Vivien appreciated the contact.

"Who are you?" she asked.

"Nurse Armstrong."

"I'm Vivien and this is Lauren, my sister."

"I know."

"How do you know?"

"Your inner voice. I hear you."

Lauren took Vivien's hand and squeezed it.

"You're a ghost," Vivien said matter of factly. "Why are you still here? In the hospital, I mean."

Beside her, Lauren barely seemed to breathe. Her stillness made Vivien look over at her.

"I want my baby," Nurse Armstrong said.

"Your baby?"

"Where is she? How can I find her?"

"I don't know. Everything is gone."

Nurse Armstrong sounded upset. Maybe she should change the conversation.

"Do you know when you died? Or why?"

Silence fell. She must be thinking. Her form, although still transparent, had settled into a more stable form, clear enough to see the watch pinned to the breast of her uniform. At first it looked like the sleeves reached down to her wrists, but now she could see the short sleeves. Her arms were also white as the cloth, along with her shoes and stockings.

Her eyes looked milky. The dark hair, caught up in a bun of some sort under the cap, framed her pale face. Her bright red lipstick glowed against the ghostly white.

"I died," the ghost said into the silence. It sounded like a remembrance rather than a statement of fact.

"You must have."

"But . . ."

"You don't remember?" Would it be strange for someone to remember dying?

"I remember going into labor. The baby was coming."

"That's the last thing you remember?" Vivien didn't know

much about babies being born, except they came from inside a mother. Too disgusting.

Lauren nudged her. "I want to go home," she whispered.

"In a minute."

"Now."

"Go on, then." Vivien felt impatient, wanting to hear what the ghost would say.

"I'm afraid."

"The baby . . ."

"What about it?"

With a sob, the ghost disappeared.

IT WAS GETTING DARK WHEN THEY GOT HOME. MAMA FUSSED ABOUT their being so late. Vivien told her they'd walked farther than she meant to, and it took longer to make the trek back. Lauren said nothing, except to look sideways at Vivien every so often.

One of the TV networks showed movies on Sunday nights, mostly old black and white films, which was okay since they only had a black and white TV. Daddy had to adjust the antenna to get a clear picture. He fussed and cussed until most of the static cleared up. Often the movie was one of Mama's romances. Daddy said he hated them, and usually laughed when they cried, and sometimes made fun of the story. This night, however, it was *Double Indemnity*, a mystery, starring Barbara Stanwyck and Fred McMurray.

Daddy seemed to be interested. He shined the brass from his uniform as he watched, the odor of Brasso drifting around them, and said not a word.

During one of the commercials, Mama made popcorn with lots of butter and salt. The smell almost cancelled out the smell of Brasso. Everyone had their own bowl and they emptied fast.

The movie ended at ten, but it was summer vacation, and the girls were allowed to stay up and watch until the end. Vivien, still preoccupied with Nurse Armstrong, decided her story must be very sad. It might make a good book, or even a movie. Maybe she would write it down.

As she lay in bed, the possibility of being a great writer, telling first the story of Nurse Armstrong, kept Vivien from sleeping. As the house quieted, and Daddy began snoring, Lauren crept into her room.

"Can I sleep with you?" she whispered.

"I guess." Vivien scooted closer to the wall and lifted the covers for her sister to slip in.

"Thanks." She put her own pillow under her head. "The nurse scared me."

"Why?"

Vivien felt her shrug. "She's a ghost. And I could see right through her."

"I told you to stay home."

"I know." Lauren lay quietly and Vivien thought she slept until she said. "You knew she was there."

"Yes, I knew. Or I knew there was something."

"Are you going back?"

"Of course."

"You're crazy."

Soon, Lauren slept, but Vivien's thoughts kept her awake. She lay still so as not to disturb her sister. When Nurse Armstrong reappeared, she felt both excited and frightened. It might be crazy to go back like Lauren said. If she didn't, though, she would never know the woman's story. And she really wanted to.

EIGHT

"Are you feeling all right?"

Mama put the back of her hand against Lauren's forehead, checking for fever, then told her younger daughter to stick out her tongue. Neither of the girls liked it when Mama checked their tongues, because if she didn't like what she saw, she gave them milk of magnesia, which tasted like chalk.

"I'm all right, Mama. I didn't sleep good. Is it okay if I just stay in bed a while longer?"

"Did you scare your sister with some story?" Mama asked Vivien, who watched from the hall.

"No, Mama."

Vivien endured Mama's questions for a few minutes, then was dismissed to go outside. Grateful to get away and fearful, she silently cursed her little sister with words she'd heard Daddy say. If Lauren told Mama about the ghost, it would mean telling her about going inside the hospital. They would be in trouble, and since Mama would tell Mrs. Moody, the boys would be in trouble. They'd never get to go back to exploring.

Little sisters! Why couldn't she be an only child?

Per and Karl hadn't come outside yet, so Vivien sat on the picnic table. She wanted to get away. If Lauren did tell, she hoped to be out of sight. Mama's anger might be gone by the time she could talk with her. Mama's scoldings hurt worse than being spanked.

The door of the trailer opened, and Mama leaned out. "Come in here, Vivien Michelle."

Oh, dear. When Mama called her by both her names, she was in big trouble. Lauren had talked.

Slowly, she climbed down from the table. Dragging her feet, she walked to the front door of the trailer. Mama held the screen door open for her and she stepped up into the living room.

"Why have you disobeyed your daddy and me? You've been inside the old hospital and now your sister is terrified. Ghosts, indeed."

"I'm sorry, Mama."

"Sorry don't cut it, my girl. You will stay here today. No hospital. No pool. No taking walks. Your daddy will hear about this." Mama took a deep breath. "Go to your room."

What room? she wanted to scream. Just a bed surrounded by three walls, which meant she lay on the bed. Her books were stacked on a shelf above the head of the bed. She didn't feel like reading. Instead, she pulled Tommy, her teddy bear, to her and hugged him.

Mama was so mad. Those few times when Vivien hurt her sister, either by hitting her, or hurting her feelings, Mama got madder at her than ever. This time could be just as bad. Or worse.

Why didn't Lauren stay home when she told her to? If she had, neither of them would be in this fix. She flopped over on her stomach and hugged the teddy bear tighter.

"Why did you tell her there was a ghost?"

Mama sat on the edge of the bed. Vivien had fallen asleep, and Mama woke her to talk. Daddy would be home soon for lunch.

"I didn't."

"You told her something?"

"I told her to stay home."

Mama got her no-nonsense look.

"The ghost just appeared."

"A real ghost."

"Yes."

Mama frowned and went into the kitchen. Vivien followed a few minutes later. Lauren sat pouting on the sofa. Plates sat on the table when Daddy drove up, but Mama went outside to talk with him first.

His eyes cut to the front door as she talked, and he looked angry. He crossed his arms, shook his head once, then nodded.

Vivien walked over to stand in front of her sister. "See what you've done."

"I'm sorry." Tears shone in Lauren's eyes and she sniffed. Vivien wouldn't let them soften her anger.

Their parents came inside.

"Sit down next to your sister," Daddy said, his voice hard. "You know what you've done." He looked directly at Vivien. "We depend on you to look after your sister when we aren't around. You did what we told you not to do, and then lied about it." She started to speak, and he held up a hand. "I don't want to hear it. You've disappointed us. Your mama and I will talk about it later and decide your punishment."

He turned away, walked back to the bathroom, and washed his hands. They all sat silently at the table. Everyone ate their sandwiches but Vivien. Her stomach churned and she could hardly swallow. Tears blurred her vision and she sniffed over and over.

Nobody spoke. Daddy finished his sandwich, kissed Mama, and left. The girls cleaned up and Mama wrapped Vivien's sandwich to put in the refrigerator.

"Go outside," she told them. "But don't go anywhere. Stay where I can see you."

"Yes, ma'am," they both said.

Vivien sat at the picnic table, contemplating the blue sky above. A slight breeze ruffled her short hair. The promise of the swimming pool lay ahead, and two months of summer and fun, yet she had never been more miserable.

For a while, Lauren sat near, but she couldn't even look at her. If the blabbermouth had just kept her mouth shut, they wouldn't be in trouble. The thought crossed her mind if she had never gone into the hospital in the first place, Lauren would never have followed and none of this would have happened.

She squelched the thought angrily. Why did she have to take care of a little sister, anyway? Damn, she wished she was an only child.

She looked around to see if Mama had come outside. Sometimes it seemed as if Mama could read her thoughts, and she frowned on cussing as one of the worst offenses. But Mama didn't appear at the door. The Moody brothers ran toward them from the other direction.

"Let's do something," Per said as he ran up to the table.

"We can't," Vivien said.

"Why not?"

"Lauren told."

Per looked from her to Lauren.

"About what?"

"About going inside the hospital," Vivien said.

"I'm sorry," Lauren said. "I didn't mean to."

"Your mama will probably tell ours."

"Probably," Vivien agreed. For a moment, the idea of sharing the punishment made her feel better.

Per shrugged and sat on the table beside her. "Our mom will probably make us stay in the house."

"How long?" Vivien asked.

"Forever. Then we won't be able to go to the pool."

"Daddy has already told us we can't go. He'll take away TV, too. I can't miss *Dragnet*."

"There are some soldiers working on getting the pool ready. I think they're Airborne." Per looked miserable. Karl stayed silent as usual, but he looked stricken.

"Really? Why would anyone from the Airborne be here?"

"They get TDY. It means 'temporary duty.'"

"I know what it means."

Per nodded. "Anyway, they say it'll be open by day after tomorrow."

"We probably won't be able to go."

Lauren looked up at her from the bench. "We have to. We worked hard to get it all cleaned up."

"No one cares. Not now."

All four bewailed the idea of not getting to use the pool. It wasn't fair. They fell silent, thinking about the horrible ways in which their parents could ruin their lives. Suddenly Mrs. Moody called to the boys to come home.

"She doesn't sound happy," Vivien said.

"Nope. Guess your mom called her."

"Sorry," Lauren said softly.

"Sure," Per said, whether in forgiveness or sarcasm she couldn't guess.

The boys started for home, dragging their feet. They disappeared inside.

"I'm so bored," Vivien said after a while.

"Yeah," Lauren said.

They both went inside and got their books. Mama glared at them and they decided reading outside would be more comfortable. The afternoon dragged on. The castaways in *Mysterious Island* discovered Captain Nemo. The story ended sadly, she thought. Vivien shook her head. Just like her own life.

"You two are grounded for the next week."

"But Daddy, the pool . . ."

"You're grounded. No pool for you two until next week. You're to stay near the house at all times, where your mama or I can see you. There will be no more visits to the hospital. Not even the Moodys' storage area."

"But what —"

"No argument. You'll need to go the library tomorrow to return your books. Make sure you get plenty more to read."

"Viv, you tell your sister there are no such things as ghosts," Mama said.

"But we *saw* her," Vivien said. Lauren nodded. "See, even she knows."

"You convinced her," Daddy said.

"No, we saw her." Vivien felt stubbornness rising. They both saw the nurse ghost and heard her speak.

Lauren stayed silent. Mama turned to her.

"You didn't see a ghost, did you?"

"No, Mama."

"Lauren!" Vivien put her hands on her hips and glared. She

felt betrayed. Her sister insisted on going with her to the hospital. Now, she said they didn't see Nurse Armstrong. How could she tell such a lie?

"Mama, we *saw* her. She's a nurse, in a white uniform. She had a baby —"

"Enough," Daddy said.

That night, Vivien lay awake and overheard them talking about her and the ghost.

"It's all the reading she does," Daddy said. "Her hormones . . . she's started her period . . . making her imagine things . . . doctor tomorrow. See what he says."

"Hysteria," Dr. Walters said the next morning.

He was an old man, at least fifty, with grey hair. His glasses sat low on his nose and he looked over them as he pronounced his diagnosis. She sat nearly naked on an examining table, wearing only underpants, so he could examine her. He touched her in ways she wasn't used to. Mama didn't say anything but watched closely.

"It happens sometimes when a young woman has her first period," he said, talking to Mama as if Vivien wasn't there. "Once her body becomes accustomed to the changes, she'll settle down."

Mama nodded and he looked over his notes. "You say she reads a lot."

"Yes."

"You might want to monitor her reading material a bit more. Too exciting or explicit material can have an effect on the young female mind."

Vivien looked over at Mama, afraid she would agree. Instead, she saw her mother's jaw twitch, a sure sign of irritation. Her parents never told her what she could or could not read, something Vivien appreciated. True, she didn't always understand adult novels, but books for younger people were mostly boring.

All the way home, Vivien hoped Mama wouldn't pay any attention to the doctor's advice about books.

The rest of the day, no one spoke about the problem. The girls each chose a book from the stack they'd checked out and sat either on the picnic table or on the sofa reading. The boys came over for a while and reported they were also confined to the immediate area, just not for as long as the girls. Once the pool opened, they would be allowed to go. They sat outside talking about how unfair life had become.

The sky grew dark with clouds before supper. Lightning streaked across the sky in the distance and thunder shook the ground. Daddy came home early. The sky continued to darken.

"We may have to leave soon," he said. His tension reached into Mama and the girls. Mama looked worried. Vivien felt frightened, yet a little excited, too. She'd never seen a tornado. They ate quickly and listened to the radio.

NINE

The trailer rocked side to side. Winds howled around the corners. Without trees, the trailer park offered no windbreak at all. The lights blinked but stayed on.

Nearby sirens nearly drowned out the weatherman's voice on TV. The warning sirens were operational now more people were living on post. Another tornado appeared in the area, but it ran to the west of them. It might hit some of the old barracks, Daddy said, but the trailer park should be safe. Vivien looked out the window trying to see the funnel but couldn't see anything in the dark.

At eleven, strong winds still rocked the trailer. The girls went to bed but neither went to sleep, and Vivien sat up when the phone rang.

"Everyone's been called into headquarters," Daddy said after a short conversation. "The twister did a lot of damage to some of the old barracks. I'll be back as soon as I can."

In a few minutes, the door closed and the Chevy drove away. So, he'd been right about the barracks.

Vivien lay awake, worrying in the darkness. From what

she'd overheard she couldn't tell how the hospital fared. She thought it must be okay since they did not hear the tornado. Mama said they sounded very loud, like freight trains.

Just then, a distant roar sounded, then faded. The wind died and the trailer stopped rocking. The storm had moved on.

The next day, Daddy hadn't come home by the time the girls got up. He was still on duty at HQ, Mama said he'd called, and she would be going to the canteen to help out. She didn't know for how long and the two of them were to stay near the trailer.

"You hear me?"

"Yes, Mama," they both said.

Daddy drove up a moment later. Mama got into the old Chevy, and they drove away. She waved as they disappeared down the road.

They cleaned up their breakfast dishes and went outside. Small tree branches, trash, and other bits of debris lay scattered on the ground, along with a small highway sign lying face down. Vivien turned it over to read it: "One Way."

"Wow!" Lauren said.

They walked around the trailer, looking to see if others were okay. Everything seemed normal, although women were outside, sweeping patios and picking up bits of stuff.

"I have to go check the hospital," Vivien said when they returned to the patio. "You stay here in case someone calls."

"But, Viv, Mama said to stay here."

"I know. But I need to make sure the . . . the building is still okay."

"But you'll get in trouble. And I'll get in trouble if I lie and they catch me."

"You owe me," Vivien said, sternly.

"But —"

"I won't be gone long."

"But —"

Vivien walked away. She didn't intend to argue with a child, especially her sister. It might not be a good idea to leave Lauren all alone, but the boys would probably come outside soon. She looked back at Lauren standing at the picnic table, her head down, looking forlorn. A pang of guilt streaked through Vivien, but she pushed it down. She had to do this.

Debris lay scattered over the road and the ground, all the way to the door, but the building itself looked undamaged.

She climbed up the stairs and opened the door, headed into the room where the ghost appeared. Which she did, even before Vivien reached the far wall.

"I've been waiting for you." Nurse Armstrong sounded angry or desperate.

"Sorry. My parents found out I've been coming here, and they grounded me."

"Grounded?"

"I haven't been allowed to leave home."

The woman nodded understanding, then fell silent.

"A tornado came close last night," Vivien said. "I came to make sure it didn't hit the hospital."

Vivien waited, shuffling her feet on the dusty floor. She had to get back home soon. Lauren couldn't be relied on to lie for her and she didn't want to risk being grounded forever.

When the silence continued, she said, "I have to go."

The ghost looked at her, squinting her milky white eyes. "Not yet."

A transparent white hand reached toward her and Vivien stepped back.

"I won't hurt you."

"I have to go home."

"I need you here."

"No, I can't . . ."

She went to the door to open it, but it stuck. She pulled harder.

"I have been learning what happened. About me, about Hans, about our baby, about . . ." She paused. "Things happened. Terrible things."

"Things happened to you?" Vivien asked, her back still to the room.

"Yes. And others."

Vivien turned to face the woman.

"Let me show you."

Pictures rolled through her mind like a movie. First, the nurse and a man in the woods, lying on a blanket. They held each other close, kissing.

"That's Hans," the nurse's voice said. The woman lying on the blanket was the nurse, now a ghost. "Such a beautiful young man."

Vivien tried to shake her head, stop the pictures, but she couldn't move. She tried to tell the ghost to let her go, but her mouth wouldn't work. And the pictures continued.

In the hospital, with people moving around, furniture and equipment in what were now empty rooms. Someone out of sight cried out in pain. A woman's voice said, "She deserves to hurt, consorting with a Kraut."

Another voice said, "Does he know?"

"Who cares," said the first voice. "There are those who would see him breathe his last."

A baby cried, the sound coming from the same direction as the earlier cries of the woman. Another nurse came into view carrying a bundle wrapped in a blanket. "It's a girl," she said.

"Best take it away, now," the first voice said.

"Can't we . . ."

"No, we won't have it here. It will be best put up for adoption, so it never knows who its father is."

The woman with the baby nodded and left.

The scene shifted. The room went dark, and Vivien wondered if it might be the same one she stood in.

"Where's my baby? I want my baby." Her voice continued to plead for her baby. No one came.

"Hans. Where is Hans? He should see his daughter."

Still, no one spoke. No one told her anything, either about her baby or its father. Soft sounds of weeping, the grief so strong that tears ran down Vivien's cheeks.

Daylight came, and the woman who became the ghost lay in a hospital bed. Her hair was damp, her eyes red. Another nurse bustled around, checking, straightening.

"My baby?"

"We told you, Lucille. Your baby died. It was cursed."

"No, don't say that. I heard it cry. Where is my daughter?"

The nurse left the room.

"I'm so sorry," Vivien said through her tears. "What happened to Hans?"

"He died under mysterious circumstances."

"You mean . . ."

"Some of the 'good' people in the area probably killed him. He went to one of the farms to work and . . ." She sighed. "He died there. Farm accident, they said."

"Did you find out where your daughter went?"

"Not then. Only recently, as a matter of fact."

"Where is she? Have you seen her?"

"Right here, now."

It took a moment to realize what the ghost said. Did she really think Vivien could be her daughter?

"No, you're wrong."

"Why else would I awaken the moment you entered this very building? I gave birth to my daughter here. I died here. Then you came. You're the right age. You have Hans's blond hair, his blue eyes."

"I have my father's hair and eyes. He's of German descent. His eyes are blue and his hair is blond. I'm not your daughter."

"Yes, you are. I know it. I feel it." The ghost drifted closer.

Vivien tried the door again, but it wouldn't budge. "I'm not your daughter," she cried as she walked to the door at the other end of the room. "I was born in Manchester, Tennessee same place as my mama. My birthday is January 18th, 1945."

She pulled on the knob of the other door as hard as she could, but it wouldn't budge. The ghost stood at one side, watching, a sweet smile on her face.

"You can't keep me here."

"I love you with all my heart, and I will never let you go."

"In here? You want to keep me in this old hospital? What will I eat? I need food and water."

Movement outside caught her eye and she stepped over to look out the window. Daddy drove past in the Chevy. Mama must be sitting beside him on the passenger's side. She pounded on the window

"Mama! Daddy!"

"They can't hear you. Soon you will forget them. You will love only me."

"But I'll die."

She knew about death. When she was younger, her grandfather died. It took a long time before Mama got over the loss of her father. Vivien remembered mostly how he smelled of tobacco and liniment. She remembered him as kind and, even though she'd only spent a matter of a few weeks with him in her life, she missed him.

She didn't want to die.

CHAPTER

TEN

Lightning flashes lit the windows and the whole building shook. Winds howled around the corners and through the cracks. Nurse Armstrong had disappeared what seemed hours ago, leaving her alone to try opening the door and windows over and over. The temperature dropped with the storm and drafts turned the room cold. Vivien huddled in a corner, shivering, exhausted.

Movement outside one of the windows caught her attention. Mama and Daddy walking to the door with Lauren. Daddy tried turning the doorknob, but he couldn't open it either. He began beating at it. With all his strength, he rammed his shoulder against it. The building shook, but the door didn't budge. They went farther down and tried there. She shouted at them not to leave. "I'm in here." She waved and beat on the windows, trying to get their attention.

No one saw her. No one heard her.

They moved farther down to the next door and she couldn't see them. She leaned close against the windows, trying to look to the left and right, but she couldn't see far enough. After a time, her family got back into the car and left without her. The last to get into the car, parked just outside the window, Lauren looked and looked at the windows, trying hard to see her big sister.

Vivien shouted her name, but with no more effect than before. In a moment, they were gone. Then she heard the sirens. Clouds gathered. The wind whipped the rain against the windows. A tornado warning? Was she safe? Was her family safe?

For a while, she continued to stand at the windows, watching lightning illuminate the buildings, reflecting from the wet road. She grew tired of standing and moved to a corner. Sliding down the wall, she sat on the floor, her arms wrapped around her knees. She leaned her forehead against her knees and cried.

When exploring the complex, the four of them realized early on that the windows were painted shut and to open them they needed something to probe the cracks. She wished now that they had brought tools to do it.

Why did Daddy not come back? He should be here, knocking down the door. Another tornado might keep him away. That must be it.

With the building shaking and rain rattling the windows, she eventually fell asleep.

SHE WOKE TO THE SOUND OF POUNDING ON THE DOOR. "VIVIEN!" Daddy shouted.

She opened her mouth to answer, but nothing came out. Clearing her throat, she tried again. Not even a squeak.

"Let's try the next door," a voice said.

No, Daddy. I'm here.

She scrambled to her feet and went to the window. Daddy stood with a man in uniform with an MP band on his arm. A military policeman. She raised her fists and pounded on the window. They would soon be out of sight. She pounded harder. The glass shattered, shards flying out onto the grass below. The sound made the men turn back. She pulled back through the hole, trying not to touch the jagged edges. Blood streaked her hand.

More pounding on the door and it finally slammed inward. Daddy ran toward her, stopped when she raised her hand.

"My god!"

The MP came up behind him.

"The window wouldn't open." She held out her hand. She realized she should be surprised she could speak now, but only felt relieved to be rescued.

Daddy pulled a handkerchief out of his back pocket and wrapped it around her hand. "There's probably some glass in the cuts," he said.

"I'll get you to the hospital," the MP said.

Daddy guided her out the door and down the steps. They got into the back seat of the patrol car and sped off, but the officer didn't turn on the siren. If she had to ride in a police car, they could at least turn on the siren.

She leaned against her father and he held her close.

"I'm sorry, Daddy."

He patted her arm. Punishment, anger, would probably come later. She knew he used anger to deal with stress. He cared but had a hard time showing it. Right then, though, he held her and remained silent. She felt safe.

Dr. Walters finished cleaning up the blood and removing a few fragments of glass from the cuts. None needed stitches. He applied Merthiolate and bandaged the whole hand to protect against infection. While he worked, Vivien told him and her father about the apparition.

"Hysteria," Dr. Walters said.

"No, she is real."

The old doctor and her father looked at her, the former with impatience, the latter with frustration, bordering on anger. They'd asked her what happened, but when she told them, they didn't let her get beyond trying to tell them about Nurse Armstrong. Dr. Walters explained to Daddy how some women just go sort of crazy when they enter puberty. "They can't handle the change in hormones," he said.

Daddy nodded in agreement.

"Bring her back in a few days. I'll start looking at the literature and see what might be the best way to treat this." He wrote down something on a sheet of paper in a folder, then stood. "In the meantime, keep her home. Don't let her go back to the old hospital." He turned to Vivien. "I know the hospital seems spooky, but there are no such things as ghosts. Go swimming, get out in the sun," the doctor continued. "Play with your friends. Stay away from the hospital." He tied the ends of a sling around her neck and helped her get her arm suspended in it. "Keep the arm up as much as you can."

Daddy helped her down from the examining table. Mama and Lauren sat in the waiting room when they came out. Silently, they left the building and got into the Chevy. Daddy had it running smoothly again. It had quite a few years behind it and sometimes wouldn't start. Daddy always said he couldn't keep the old thing running forever, no matter how good a mechanic he was.

She tried to concentrate on the mundane problem of the

car and its periodic need for repair. But everything else kept creeping into her mind. If they didn't believe in the ghost, they would never believe the scene of the birth, or the taking away of the baby.

Did the people kill Hans? How did Lucille die?

She stopped a moment. How did she know the nurse's name? She'd only said her name: Nurse Armstrong. Did the nurse from the memory — the one who talked like she hated Lucille — did she say the name? Yes, she remembered.

They reached home and everyone got out. "Fix yourself some Cheerios," Mama said, then went outside to talk with Daddy. Vivien felt hungry and she wolfed down a whole bowl of cereal and milk in what seemed like seconds. She poured milk on a second bowl when Mama walked back inside. Through the window, she saw the car pulling away, Daddy heading back to work. Very little interfered with his dedication to being a soldier.

Mama shooed Lauren outside and sat down at the table with her elder daughter. Vivien's appetite waned, and she ate slowly, needing to do something other than just sit and feel Mama looking at her.

"Is what you told the doctor the whole story?"

Vivien looked up then. Trust Mama to sense there was more.

"No, ma'am."

"Tell me everything."

The story began slowly, starting from the beginning. Mama sat with her hands flat on the tabletop, listening, asking no questions.

At the part where the ghost said Vivien was her daughter, she began speaking faster. Like many of her friends, she sometimes wished she'd been adopted. Usually when Mama and Daddy punished her for some infraction of the rules she saw as unfair. Being adopted didn't seem such a good idea now, with Nurse Armstrong claiming her as her daughter.

When she finished telling the events of the night, and how much it scared her, Mama held her good hand and sat silently, thinking. She spoke slowly, as if she didn't want to say the words.

"Some things can only be understood by seeing it or hearing it. Things not even the books and magazines you read can teach you."

Vivien frowned, surprised. Mama knew what books she read. Every so often, Vivien used her allowance to buy movie magazines, which she shared with Mama, and sometimes with Lauren, exacting a promise from her little sister she would be careful and not tear them. She stored them in a cardboard box under her bed, most in near pristine condition. They were a shared experienced among the three of them.

"What do you mean? You believe me?"

Mama went to the stove and poured herself a cup of coffee. She added sugar and cream, while Vivien finished the cereal. She placed her bowl in the sink, then sat back down. Mama joined her at the table, her forehead wrinkled in thought.

"How's your hand?"

"It hurts some. Mama, will I have to take some kind of medicine? Doctor Walters said —"

"We'll see. Now go outside with your sister."

Outside, Vivien grabbed up the deck of cards Lauren took out and started playing solitaire on the picnic table. The boards were warped, making it difficult to lay the cards in a perfect row.

"Let me play, too," Lauren said. She'd been waiting at the table.

"What do you want to play?"

"Double solitaire?"

"Okay."

She gathered up the cards and shuffled them. As she dealt them out, the Moody boys came running outside.

"You're okay," Per said when he got to the table.

"Yeah."

"What happened? Did you stay inside the hospital all night?"

"Yeah."

"Wow". He bounced from foot to foot. Karl sat next to Lauren, without a word, as usual, staring at Vivien. She wondered what made him so solemn most of the time.

Vivien hesitated to talk about it. But she realized she might need Per's help to find out about Lucille Armstrong and her boyfriend, Hans.

She told them all about going to the hospital to see the ghost and the ghost's name. She went on to tell them about the nurse not letting her out, but not the truth about why.

"I guess she's lonely." She told them Lucille had a German POW for a boyfriend. "She got sick and died, I guess. She thought Hans died, too."

"Tell her about the cemetery," Karl said.

"There's a cemetery?" Vivien asked.

"Yeah, but we don't know where," Per said. "We heard the POWs who died are buried there."

"Do you think you can find out from your dad where it is?" she asked.

"Maybe. But not if you are the one who wants to know."

"You don't have to tell anyone."

"He'll probably guess."

"Don't you have a map of the whole post? Maybe your daddy has one."

"Yeah." He seemed apprehensive about where the conversation might take them. Vivien had assumed he would be excited about a new adventure. For nearly a month now, the four of them had been all over the hospital complex and the post, free as birds, making up stories as they went along.

After a moment's thought, he said, "I'll get it. If I can get out of the house without Mom seeing."

He ran over to his house, disappearing inside. Vivien scooped up the cards and shuffled them over and over as they waited. Per reappeared, carrying a stack of books, which he dropped on the table.

"I told Mom we all wanted something to read." He opened one of the larger books and pulled out the map. "Here it is."

They spread it out, putting books on the corners to hold them down. It took a long moment for them to orient themselves.

"This is the trailer park." Per placed his index finger on the spot. "The pool . . . is at this end. These are the woods behind the pool." His hand moved across the trailer park location. "This is the hospital."

"Would the cemetery be near the hospital?" Vivien asked.

Per shrugged. "Who knows."

She scanned the map, all the while wondering what symbol might have been used to indicate a cemetery. She imagined a cross or a small tombstone. When she found it, a cross marked the spot, nowhere near the hospital.

"Here it is."

Per looked closely. "It's in the woods behind the pool."

ELEVEN

"You can go to the pool, but only for two hours and only for Lauren's swimming lessons."

Lauren couldn't go unless Mama or Vivien went to watch over her. Mama kept busy in the house and with Vivien's being grounded, she couldn't go either. Lauren declared that totally unfair. Daddy finally agreed Vivien could go to the pool.

Vivien could splash about as long as she didn't get her bandaged hand wet. It wouldn't be long, before her hand healed. What she really wanted to do was to search for the cemetery. In order to do that, she asked Per and Karl to keep an eye on her sister.

"But we want to search for it, too," Per said.

"I don't want you and Karl to get in trouble because of me," she told him. "And Lauren can't go since she has swimming lessons."

"So do you," Lauren reminded her.

Vivien held up her injured hand. "Not until this is all healed. I'll ask Walt if he'll teach me later, once I can get in the water. If you three are there, while I'm in the woods, there's less chance I'll be missed."

Vivien had only heard about Walt, one of the two lifeguards at the pool, from the others, since she hadn't been to the pool, yet. The two young men were in the Airborne division stationed at Fort Campbell, on temporary assignment to the summer camp. Walt offered to teach the kids how to swim and about water safety.

Per declared her plan made sense. Lauren pouted and wouldn't speak to Vivien.

Her plan nearly fell apart when she met Walt, the lifeguard, whom the others had already met during her two days "confined to quarters," as Daddy phrased her punishment. He had black hair, wore a black bathing suit, stood at least six feet tall, and his smile melted her heart. For the first time, in her young life, she fell in love.

"Girls are so silly," Per said, noticing her gaze follow the lifeguard.

"I'm not a girl. I'm a young woman."

Why didn't he see how perfectly wonderful Walt was? In the pool, he swam like a fish. His smile made her stomach flutter. His voice sounded like music. Vivien dredged up every description she'd ever heard in a movie. Plus, being nineteen or twenty made him a man, not a boy.

More than ever, she wished she could start the swimming lessons. Spending time with him nearly became more important than searching the woods. She felt sure he would give her special attention as he taught them all about swimming, and how to save themselves and others should anything happen.

Difficult as it was, she tore herself away after the hour and headed into the woods. She shivered in the shade of trees and overgrown bushes. Blackberry brambles caught at her bathing suit and scratched her legs as she worked her way deeper into the tangle.

On the map, the cross indicating the cemetery lay to the right and ahead, but she had no idea how far. In the claustrophobic atmosphere, she could be just a few feet from it and not know it. She figured there would be a clear area, but in the tangle of vegetation she could easily walk right past it.

When she tired of fighting vines and bushes, she turned back, sure the lessons had ended by now. Emerging into sunlight, she took a moment to let her eyes adjust. She located Lauren and Karl splashing in the shallow end of the pool. She couldn't see Per at first, then saw him crossing the deep end. Already a good swimmer, he wanted to learn lifesaving techniques from Walt. The lifeguard stood near the edge, watching.

As casually as she could, she walked around the end of the pool, approaching Walt, while her heart beat fast and the bottom of her stomach fell out. "Hi, I'm Vivien. I was wondering . . . w-would you teach me in a few days, when my hand heals?"

"Sure." He smiled down at her. "Just let me know when you're ready."

She could feel herself blushing and turned away. Holding the wrapped hand above her head, she jumped into the shallow end, splashing Lauren and Karl. They all laughed and kept splashing each other for a minute or two, until Lauren decided she wanted to practice saving Vivien. It was awkward, to say the least.

Lauren had become a strong but awkward swimmer. She struggled to learn the techniques of the rescue part. Vivien's wounded hand didn't help, and when she tried swimming, using only one arm, a few wet spots appeared on the bandages. They gave up for the moment.

"I need to get home." She'd asked for the time from one of the mothers sitting beside the pool.

"I want to stay," Lauren whined. "Per and Karl are here."

"Daddy said —"

"Please let me stay."

Vivien looked over at Karl who nodded. Vivien told him to get Per so he could watch Lauren, too. She pushed herself onto the apron of the pool, grabbed her towel, and started running home, the flip-flops slapping against her heels. Having gone a short way, she stopped. The hair stood up on the back of her neck, a feeling she got when someone looked at her without her seeing them. She turned around. No one at the pool looked her way. They watched others swim, or sunned themselves in lounge chairs, their eyes closed.

A shiver went through her again, and she looked around the trailer park. Seeing nothing, she shrugged it away.

<hr>

"You're late."

"I know. We were practicing saving each other."

"We?"

Mama reached for the bandaged hand. A couple of drops had left wet spots.

"Didn't someone have a watch?"

"Yes. We just . . ."

"We'll let it go this time. But you'll have to do better."

"Yes, Mama."

Vivien went into the bathroom, took off her wet bathing suit, and hung it up to dry. After drying herself with a towel, she changed into halter top and shorts, and went back into the living room.

Mama dusted furniture preparatory to running the

vacuum. One of the best ways to get on her good side would be to help without being asked. Vivien grabbed a rag and started dusting the built-in shelves where knick-knacks and books were kept.

"What's on your legs?"

Vivien looked down to see red scratches from the brambles. For a moment, she panicked. Thinking fast, she finally said, "I went in the woods behind the pool. I thought I saw some blackberry vines." Mama had pointed out some one day when Daddy drove them around the post, so she knew what they looked like.

"Oh?"

"There are lots of them, but not so many berries. Maybe I should take a bucket tomorrow and pick some."

"It's too early. They won't be ripe before next month."

Darn. She thought she'd found the perfect excuse for going into the woods again.

They finished the dusting and Mama let her do some of the vacuuming.

Mama hadn't taught her to do the ironing, yet, but she'd learned to do a few other grownup chores. So far, she didn't much like doing most of them, but as a girl, it would be her responsibility when she grew up.

Mama fixed them each a glass of iced tea when they finished cleaning, and they went outside. Vivien sat on the picnic table as usual, setting down the aluminum glass Mama loved so much. The outside of it sweat and made her hand wet. She hated that.

Mama sat in one of the metal lawn chairs wiping at the beads of moisture on her own glass with her index finger. Both were just barely in the shade of the trailer. They sat quietly, Mama fanning herself with the magazine she brought outside to read. Even the birds were quiet in the heat. Every so often shouts from the pool wafted to them on a breeze.

Soon, Mrs. Warner joined them, pulling the other lawn chair into the shade. She and Mama talked about usual things, then grew quiet.

"I wondered if I could borrow Vivien after lunch for some help inside," Mrs. Warner said. "I'm sorting through a few things we brought back from Japan."

"All right with me," Mama said. "Vivien?"

She had just been wondering what she could do to keep from being so bored. She had once seen some of the treasures from Japan and helping to sort through the collection would be fun.

"The little window air conditioner should have it a bit cooler soon," Mrs. Warner said. She stood and led the way to her trailer.

"It's beautiful."

Vivien held a paper fan with a white-on-white design. She'd opened it out being careful not to tear it.

"It's not delicate," Mrs. Warner said. "The Japanese make such things to be used."

Vivien fanned herself with it, enjoying the breeze it stirred up, then folded it carefully.

"You have so many beautiful things." She sat on the living room rug with the array of items spread out around her. "They're all from Japan?"

"Most of it. Some in other places, like this ivory Buddha, we got in Hong Kong." Mrs. Warner placed it gently in her hand.

"It must be terribly expensive."

"If you bought one here in the States, it would be." She

handed Vivien a pad of lined paper. "I want to make a list of everything and where I bought it. I'll tell you what it is, and you write it down. As clearly as you can."

Vivien felt proud of what teachers called her "hand," a word they used for handwriting. She practiced a lot, especially signing her name.

"We can start with the Buddha. It's a small ivory Buddha, carved in China, bought in Hong Kong." She spelled "Buddha" for Vivien.

They discussed exactly how she wanted it written down in columns: Buddha, Chinese, Hong Kong, value. It eliminated superfluous words.

Next, a jade bead necklace. And so on, with the older woman spelling the foreign words.

"Daddy hopes we'll be sent to Japan next. He's due an overseas post."

"You'd love it." Mrs. Warner sat looking at her thoughtfully. "I hear you've seen a ghost."

"Who . . . Mama . . .?"

"Yes. She's worried about you."

"Doctor Walters thinks I'm imagining it. He says starting . . . I mean . . ."

"I know about that, too."

Of course, she did. She drove her and Mama to the store. Still, Vivien's face grew hot. Would she always be embarrassed by this thing a woman had to do to grow up? Mama said it was perfectly natural, yet she shouldn't talk about it.

"Men don't understand what women's bodies go through," Mrs. Warner said. "I think it scares some of them. Many women don't understand, either. But . . ." Mrs. Warner shrugged, looking thoughtful again. "I can say with perfect assurance it has nothing to do with your seeing a ghost."

"Really?"

"Of course."

"But the doctor."

"He may be a doctor, but he's as ignorant of women's bodies as any other man. Well, almost. We grow up, we grow older, same as men. But we are very different. We are the ivory." She picked up the Buddha. "They are the brass." She picked up a small metal dish. "Tell me about your ghost."

Vivien hesitated. No one believed her. She worried about the whole thing, and curious about the woman and what her life had been. It made her search for the cemetery.

She started with how she and the others explored the hospital, even though they weren't supposed to. Mrs. Warner said nothing, except to ask a few questions as she listened. Vivien told of going there alone, and how the nurse trapped her in the building.

"I saw what looked like a memory of her baby being taken away. The nurses with her when she gave birth didn't like her much." Another memory came to her. "I remember now. The nurse told Lucille her baby died."

"Why didn't they like her?"

"I think because the father of her baby was a German soldier."

"Did you see her die?"

Vivien shook her head. She finished telling about being trapped in the building. She looked down at her hand as she explained about trying to get her father's attention next morning.

"We think the POW cemetery is in the woods behind the pool. I couldn't find it this morning, but I didn't have much time to look."

"Ghosts are nothing to fool around with," Mrs. Warner said when she finished.

"You believe me?"

"Oh, yes. Although I must say this doesn't sound like a typical haunting. This Lucille Armstrong is like many ghosts who died mysteriously or unhappily. No one's happy about dying, but the nurse being young and having just given birth, she must have been terribly unhappy. Her thinking you are her daughter is more than a little strange."

"They told her the baby died." Being able to talk about what happened with someone who took her seriously excited her.

"Usually ghosts know exactly what happened to them, and in a case like this, she would know what happened to the baby, probably even know where it is now."

"Even if it died?"

"Yes. Although she might not want to accept it."

"She's so sure her baby lived."

"You did say you woke her?"

"She said I did. She said I must be her daughter because she awakened when I entered the room."

"And she didn't remember some things at first." Vivien nodded. "What did she say about Hans?"

"He died in a farm accident."

"Such accidents were pretty commonplace. But under those circumstances . . ."

"What?"

"If everyone in the area knew he fathered Lucille's baby, they might have been angry at him. He could have been murdered."

TWELVE

Murdered. Why did Mrs. Warner think someone killed Hans?

They continued cataloguing the items and discussing the facts as known about the nurse and her lover, as Mrs. Warner called him. "I don't think you should go back to the hospital," she said. "Although most ghosts are harmless, Lucille seems very angry. We can't tell what she might do."

"How do you know so much about ghosts?"

"My grandmother did. She taught me a lot, including how to convince an unsettled one to leave a house or wherever they might be haunting."

"Where else would they haunt?"

"Oh, churches, a lot of them. Babies won't leave their nurseries, sometimes. Children. I knew of one who haunted the school playground where he died."

"Do they always haunt the places where they die?"

"Not always. Sometimes they haunt the place where they were happiest."

"So, Nurse Armstrong died in the hospital just as she showed me."

"Most likely."

"If we found the place where Hans died, would his ghost be there? I thought he might be at his grave."

"You aren't thinking of looking for him, are you?" Mrs. Warner caressed the jade figure they had just put on the list.

"Maybe he knows what happened to their baby."

"Why? Do you want to tell her, so she won't think you're her daughter? Or out of curiosity?"

Vivien thought about it. The ghost frightened her. But she felt sorry for her, too. If she really did just find out her daughter died all those years ago, her sadness would be more now than if she'd always known. Nonetheless, she had the feeling the ghost wouldn't give up. Nor would Vivien. She didn't like to be scared.

Vivien couldn't express all those thoughts easily. But Mrs. Warner understood what was happening more than she did.

"I'm not afraid, but maybe I can help Lucille find out about her baby. She might go back to sleep if she knows."

"I understand your wanting to help her rest in peace, so to speak. But she could be dangerous. Don't get yourself involved in something you can't control."

Vivien promised and they turned their full attention on listing all the items they'd set out on the dining table and coffee table. In the end, there were forty-three items. They must be worth hundreds of dollars.

The clock on the stove said it five o'clock. Time to get home for dinner.

"Let me give you something for all this work," Mrs. Warner said.

"That's all right. I enjoyed it."

"I'm glad you enjoyed it, but still, you should have some

payment. How about —" her hand moved above the items, "— the fan you listed first?"

"Oh, no. It's worth a fortune."

"Not that much. And you seemed to like it."

"I do. It's beautiful. But . . ."

"It's settled. Tell your mother I gave it to you, and I thank her for letting you come over."

"Yes, ma'am."

The fan was wrapped in a protective sleeve and Vivien pulled it free and opened it. A shiver of a thrill at its beauty ran through her. It had elegance and adultness about it.

"Thank you."

"You're welcome. And, dear, don't tell your mother we talked about the ghost. She won't approve of my — well — encouraging you."

Vivien nodded. "I know. I won't say anything."

"Good."

Mrs. Warner thanked her again as she left.

***

"No!"

Vivien sat up in bed, wakened by her own shout. Daddy called her name from his bedroom. She stayed silent and lay back, hoping he would believe she cried out in her sleep. She held her breath, but her lungs were desperate for air. Her heart pounded. She wiped sweat from her forehead with the edge of the sheet.

The trailer still hadn't cooled down from the afternoon heat. Even the babydoll pajamas were too warm. She sat up and waited. When she heard Daddy snoring again, she crept out of bed. Tiptoeing in bare feet, she managed to open the front door and slip outside with only the slightest sound.

It was a little cooler than inside, and she knew mosquitoes would be aiming at her already, but she couldn't go back inside. She took two deep breaths, then looked straight up at the stars. No moon shone to brighten the sky, and the streetlights were too few to drown out the light show overhead.

Calmer now, she moved to the picnic table and sat on top with her feet on the bench as usual. She leaned back on her hands and looked over at the hospital. The dream came back to her.

She walked from room to room, trying to find something. Getting out didn't worry her. She had the sense she couldn't get out, so no use in trying. Something else made her hurry through the corridors and rooms, searching. She knew what she wanted and where to find it. At the other end of the complex.

What she needed to find so badly was Lauren.

THIRTEEN

Vivien watched Lauren splash in the pool. She hated to admit she loved her little sister and would fight anyone to keep anything from happening to her. But how does one fight a ghost?

The dream from the night before remained vivid in her mind. The fear for her sister, the lack of air in the hospital. Lauren was safe, but the fear still made her heart beat faster.

Vivien sighed and jumped into the pool. Walt helped a girl who looked to be closer to his age. A pang of jealousy soured her anticipation of today's swimming lesson. He smiled down at the girl, then walked over to where the kids waited.

Why would a man like Walt be interested in a kid, anyway? In spite of her newfound womanhood, he must think of her as being too young. A child.

There were some new students this morning, making a total of seven. He always started out with floating on the water. He worked with the three new kids. Everyone else could do it well now, except for Vivien. For some reason, she couldn't float. He didn't know why, either. She lay back like the others, and immediately her butt sank, folding her in two like a jack knife as she struggled to stay on top of the water. Walt came to her and put his hand on her lower back and lifting, she floated. Until he let go.

"We'll get this yet," he said. "I think maybe you're too stiff."

Next, he showed them how to bounce off the bottom of the pool and make their way to the edge. They sank, reached the bottom, bent their knees, then pushed themselves to the surface. A gulp of air, down, bounce, air. All the while getting closer to the opposite edge.

"Under some circumstances," he said, "you can save yourself."

He lined them up against one side of the pool, their backs against the concrete wall. He told them to put their feet against it and push off with their hands stretched out in front of them and their faces in the water. They tried to go farther each time by just kicking their feet. Vivien got nearly halfway across the pool before having to put her head up for a breath. To her surprise, Lauren didn't stop, raising her head a moment later.

Dumb sister.

The lesson ended, and they were free to play. She went to the shallow end and walked up the steps onto the concrete apron. Grabbing her towel, she wrapped it around her, using the corners to get the water out of her ears. She looked for the girl Walt had been talking to but didn't see her.

Both lifeguards talked with other swimmers. She nodded to Per, who knew where she intended to go, and slipped on her flip-flops. She walked toward the woods as casually as an eleven-year-old girl can, with one glance back to see if anyone else noticed. Lauren watched, a frown on her face. Vivien ignored her, turned, and walked into the woods.

The coolness in the shade surprised her again. She shivered and pulled the towel around her shoulders.

She started out more to the left than the first few times. A few feet into the brush, she picked up a long stick to part the vines and bushes. Something out of sight to the right rustled the dead leaves and she stopped. After waiting a minute, she saw nothing, no movement of undergrowth. She continued, finding the going easier than the day before.

After a moment, she saw a path meandered deeper through the tangle, only slightly blocked by the undergrowth. It could mean the cemetery lay in this direction. Why else would a path be here?

When she stepped into the burial ground, she didn't realize it at first. Even there, vines and briers covered the ground, only less so than the surrounding area.

She stumbled, caught her balance with the stick. Looking down, she saw a small metal plaque sticking upright from the ground. She stooped down, trying to read it, but couldn't make out the words. Other plaques, dark with age and dirt, were impossible to read in the shade.

With both hands, she pulled at the first one, found she could get her hands under the horizontal part. Rocking it back and forth, it gave way suddenly, and she fell back, hands clutching the treasure.

On close inspection, it proved to be a rectangular piece made of iron and more than a little rusted. Two prongs on both corners of the bottom were long enough to make it difficult to pull the thing free. However, the ground was soft, almost spongy, with damp and the working of multiple roots.

She found a patch of sunlight shining through a gap in the trees and bushes overhead and held the plaque in it, moving it to read the whole thing. She ran her fingertips over the raised letters, trying to clean them.

It read "Gunter Schmidt."

She'd found the POW cemetery.

She looked around to identify the boundaries and noticed the vegetation grew more sparsely here than she originally thought. She took the metal piece in her hand and pushed it back into the ground. The grave markers stood side by side, with a small space between. The graves themselves must be very narrow.

She read three before finding the one she wanted: "Hans Koch." Below the name: "Died 1944." No date, no birthdate, no age like she'd seen on her grandfather's gravestone. She found it very sad.

Knowing he died while a POW might be interesting, but how did it help with Nurse Armstrong? As she wondered, she turned the plaque over and over in her hand. Eventually, her fingers detected raised letters on the back side.

Once more she held it up in the sliver of sunlight that had moved slightly since finding the first grave marker. She tracked the smaller letters with her fingertips as she read it.

"Beloved husband and father."

Did it mean he and Lucille were married? Or did he have a wife back in Germany? Where in Germany? How could she find out? Old records from twelve years ago?

The library. If there were papers, records, anything, maybe the library would have them.

"We have very few records of the post and a only few on the prisoners of war."

Mrs. Finfrock, the librarian tried to help her find the information she sought, but there didn't seem to be much in the library. Most records would be with the Army, she said, maybe a few things in the headquarters building.

How in the world would Vivien ever be able to see those?

"Where could I find out about marriage licenses?"

If Lucille and Hans did get married, it would probably have been in town.

"Those records are kept at city hall," Mrs. Finfrock said. "I don't remember there being many weddings with the soldiers, though."

"How long have you lived here?"

"All my life."

"Did you know any of the POWs? I'm trying to find information on a Hans Koch. Or a nurse named Lucille Armstrong."

The librarian's eyes widened, and her expression became stern. "How do you know those names?"

Her voice, so sharp, made Vivien lean back from the desk.

"I heard someone talking about them. They said there was a romance, and they had a baby, but they all died."

"I don't know anything about that."

"Do you at least know if they got married?"

"No, they did not." The librarian pushed Vivien's stack of books she'd checked out toward her and turned away.

Vivien picked up the stack. "Thanks, Mrs. Finfrock."

It was Saturday and the whole family were in town to do the shopping. Lauren decided to go with Mama to the grocery store and Daddy planned to buy a new pair of shoes. He gave Vivien money to get an ice cream or soda after visiting the library and to be back at the car in an hour and half. The town clock, in the tower of city hall, showed she still had an hour before then.

She stopped a woman walking along the sidewalk to ask how to find the newspaper office. The woman told her around the corner. Vivien walked in to find yet another older woman, Mrs. Brooks according to the sign, behind a desk.

"May I help you?"

"Yes, ma'am. Do you keep old papers in here?"

"How old?"

"1944."

The woman confirmed they had them for that year. A short time later, Vivien sat at a table deeper in the offices with scrapbooks both on the table and on shelves along one wall. The room had no windows and the two lamps on the table cast only a dim glow.

The newspaper had been in existence for over thirty years and back issues were carefully stored in the room. She opened the book for 1944 the woman set on the table for her. With the scarcity of paper during the war, Mrs. Brooks explained as she set out the book, the newspaper had only come out twice a week. Once the war ended, they returned to a daily issue.

The wall clock showed she had nearly forty-five minutes left. The woman had warned her some of the papers were fragile with age and asked her to be careful. The paper was stronger than the woman led her to believe. She turned the pages slowly, first checking the obituaries, but found nothing in that column. Next, she scanned the pages for any mention of the camp, POWs, or nurses. Some of the headlines were tricky, but it took only a moment to determine whether any were important to her search.

A headline from the middle of March caught her eye: *German Soldier dies in freak accident.*

Vivien grabbed a pencil from a cup on the table and a piece of loose note paper, noted down the date —— March 14, 1944 — then read the story. *Hans Koch, aged 23, a German POW being held at Camp Breckinridge, died in a farm accident last Thursday. When driving the farm's tractor up an incline, the machine rolled over, crushing him underneath. He is reportedly survived by a wife and child who live in Stuttgart, Germany. He will be buried in the POW cemetery at Breckinridge. No services will be held.*

She noted down the few details. So, he was married when he met Nurse Armstrong. Did she know? How strange his death didn't show up in the obituaries. Also, strange neither the farm nor the farmer was named. Maybe everyone in the area knew where he worked.

Before her imagination got the better of her, she turned more pages, moving into April, then May. The next thing catching her eye wasn't a headline at all but an item under birth announcements: *Daughter born to Lucille Armstrong, unwed mother, at Breckinridge Army Hospital. Both died soon after birth.*

The date, May 7, 1944. Again, no mention in the obituaries of either death.

Vivien turned back to March and looked at headlines more closely. She came upon an article which puzzled her. It reported a police investigation into an incident that occurred on March 14 in which a small group of men attacked and killed a man. At trial several days later, the judge who heard the case ruled everyone innocent, citing the lack of witnesses. The injured party was not named, but the men charged were Grady Nelson, Darren Grant, Michael Ford, John Vincent. She stopped and stared at the last name, Gerald Finfrock.

FOURTEEN

Per and Vivien sat together on the edge of the pool and dangled their legs in the water. She had told him what she found in the newspapers and how Mrs. Finfrock had acted strangely when asked about Lucille and Hans. Vivien guessed Gerald Finfrock must be her husband. Which probably meant Mrs. Finfrock not only didn't want to talk about it but would be angry if asked any more questions.

"Yeah," Vivien said. "It's a small town. Everybody knows everybody. The people probably resented the German prisoners. Those articles about a man dying. Was it two men dying on the same day? The reporter didn't give the name of the man in the article on the trial."

"What does that mean?"

"What if it's a coverup like in the movies?"

"How?"

"Well, say Lucille's Hans was murdered and the murder was discovered. The sheriff arrested those men right away. Everyone decided Hans deserved to die, and they make up the story about the tractor turning over."

Per laughed. "You should write a movie or something."

Vivien pouted, stung by his comment. "It's possible," she said.

"Why would they want to kill him?"

"He was a German soldier. He had a wife in Germany and he was courting Nurse Armstrong. That's a pretty bad thing to do."

"I don't understand why they would kill him for that," he said. "I mean, sure, he shouldn't have been with Nurse Lucille when he already had a wife back in Germany. But what difference did it make to them?"

"Maybe because he was a Kraut and they didn't like him dating an American."

They sat contemplating all she had learned, most of which they found confusing. Mama always said she had too vivid an imagination and knew more than an eleven-year-old should. Vivien realized what she knew she didn't always understand. She also knew her curiosity sometimes made grownups uncomfortable.

Vivien adjusted the wide-brimmed straw hat Mama insisted she wear against the hot sun because of her sunburnt nose. Only a few people were in the pool, including Karl and Lauren who would have stayed in the water every hour of the day if they could. They would all have to go home for lunch soon.

Vivien no longer felt she wanted to venture into the woods again. The more she found out, the more confused she became. Unless the dreams stopped. She couldn't remember most of them, only much how they frightened her.

Since the pool opened, none of them had gone back into the hospital. Nurse Armstrong had only appeared there, and Vivien hoped by staying away to never see her again. However, when she remembered the details in the newspapers, she couldn't help feeling sorry for her. Losing her baby, and the man she must have loved, would make anyone sad. Did she know about his wife and child in Germany?

While she and her friends walked home for lunch, she knew she needed to tell the ghost what she'd found out. To do so, she would have to go back to the hospital. But the thought of going frightened her. Anyway, Mama and Daddy wouldn't let her. Of course, she could find a way if she really wanted to.

Could she find some way to protect herself from Nurse Armstrong? Maybe Mrs. Warner knew how. But if she went to her, she'd tell her not to go. She must find a way to let the ghost know about her lover and child.

CHAPTER
FIFTEEN

Vivien drifted awake. Her face felt warm and damp. All the windows of the trailer were open, but no breeze stirred the short curtains. She suffered from the heat more than anyone else in the family. In summer, she got little sleep some nights and woke crabby the next morning.

She threw off the sheet, hoping to cool off. It didn't help. She blew on her right arm and the dampness of her skin, raised goose bumps.

Her mind wandered from her discomfort to memories of the day before, one scene to another. A vague unease settled on her about what woke her. A sound or touch. Not the dream. Something else there, she couldn't remember.

She sat up and new goose bumps popped up. She shivered in suddenly cool air.

The soles of her feet pressed against the cool floor when she slipped out of bed. She padded into Lauren's bedroom, between hers and their parents'. Her night-tuned eyes revealed her little sister's empty bed.

She moved on to the bathroom. No one there, either

In the back bedroom, Daddy snored loudly.

She parted the curtains on the small window opposite Lauren's bed, trying to see if Lauren might be at the picnic table on the patio. It sat too far to the right to see all of it.

Vivien got dressed and, holding her flip-flops in her hand, she slipped outside. She looked around as she put them on. Instinct told her to check the pool.

She ran down the road, the soft sandals slapping against her heels. Lauren wouldn't go there in the middle of the night, would she? Too much imagination Daddy would say. But it wasn't true. Vivien had always been able to find lost items, or known the phone would ring before it did. When Lauren ran away once before, she found her hiding exactly where she expected — in the woods within sight of their house.

This felt the same. And she ran under the light from the stars, and the occasional streetlight, knowing the road so well, afraid she might be too late.

She reached the pool, breathing hard. Lauren floated face down in the water.

"Lauren!"

Vivien pulled off her sandals, took a deep breath and jumped in. Warm water caressed her skin. She bobbed to the surface and swam quickly to her sister's side.

"Who . . .?" A man's voice called out.

"Help!" She turned Lauren's small body over and started pulling her to the side of the pool. A splash and stronger hands took over. Because of the run and the fear, Vivien gasped for breath. She let the man take the small body in his arms.

They climbed out awkwardly. Only then did she recognize Walt. Movement at the deep end of the pool caught her eye. The girl he'd talked to the other day, stood, watching. She ran her fingers through her disheveled hair and pulled down her blouse. All of this Vivien saw in a fraction of a second. Her attention went back to Lauren, lying so still on the concrete apron, her wet pajamas clinging to her.

Walt turned Lauren onto her stomach and pushed on her back, trying to get the water from her lungs. In a moment Lauren coughed up water and spluttered. She tried to sit up, but Walt held her down.

"What are you two doing here in the middle of the night?" He looked from one to the other, angrily.

"I just got here," Vivien said.

At the same time Lauren asked, "Where?"

Out of the corner of her eye, Vivien saw the older girl turn away and leave, probably for home.

She looked at Walt, tears gathering in her eyes. She sniffed them back and turned to sit beside her sister, rubbing her back, like Mama did whenever one of them didn't feel good. "Why did you come to the pool?"

"I didn't."

"Did someone bring you here?" Walt asked.

"I don't remember."

"You don't remember being in the water?" he asked.

Lauren shook her head. She looked about to cry.

"Did you come with her?" he asked, turning his attention to Vivien.

"I woke up and looked for her. I had the feeling she would be here, so I ran all the way."

"You thought she'd be here?" He had been on his knees, and he now sat cross legged. "I don't understand."

"I had the feeling I'd find her at the pool and in trouble."

He shook his head. "I guess sisters are like that." He looked over his shoulder at the pool shed. He must have been in there when she shouted. "Looks like you saved your sister's life," he said, turning back to her. "You were very brave."

"Thanks. I'm glad you were here."

Accusation tinged her voice and she really wanted to ask, "Why were you here?" But she didn't. The important thing was that Lauren didn't drown.

HE STOOD AND HELPED THEM BOTH TO THEIR FEET. "I'LL MAKE SURE you two get home," he told them, and took Vivien's hand. He wore slacks and a golf shirt instead of the usual swimsuit. His touch made her stomach quiver, something she had never felt.

She protested they could get home all right, but he insisted. "I should talk to your parents.

They begged him not to, especially Lauren, nearly in tears all over again. "They won't let me come to the pool if you tell them," she cried.

"We'll see," he said. "The important thing is you're okay." In the end, he watched them go inside and walked away.

They slipped through the door and Vivien helped her sister get into dry pajamas. "We'll talk tomorrow," she said.

"Don't tell Mama," Lauren begged. "She won't ever let me go to the pool again if you do."

"I won't. But we have to make sure it doesn't happen again."

Lauren nodded. She must be more frightened of losing pool privileges than of what had happened.

Vivien changed into her own pajamas and crawled into bed. Having been outside, she felt cooler, but before long the heat in the trailer made her throw off the sheet again. Questions and the heat wouldn't let her sleep.

What did happen? Who or what drew her little sister to the pool in the middle of the night?

How could Lauren have gotten out of the trailer without her hearing? She had to walk right past Vivien's bed to get to the front door. Vivien slept so lightly every sound during the night, every vibration of the trailer woke her. Why didn't she hear Lauren go outside?

For once, she was grateful at not being able to fall asleep. Lauren's little adventure made her want to stay awake, listening and watching. And the questions kept coming.

Had Lauren just walked in her sleep? She'd never done it before, but this summer, everything seemed to be changing. And the excitement of the pool and their freedom to roam about at will, made each day a new experience.

The one question she pushed down over and over: Did Nurse Lucille have anything to do with what happened? After her locking Vivien in the building and the ominous words about her family, she couldn't help but wonder.

By early morning Vivien finally fell sound asleep.

SIXTEEN

"Snake!"

One of the mothers screamed and pointed at something in the pool. Walt ran up. Everyone in the pool scrambled out with lots of screaming and splashing. Chris, the second lifeguard, grabbed the scoop net they used to get leaves and other trash out. The snake wriggled, trying to get away, making it difficult to capture.

Finally, he had it corralled. It looked small enough to get through the mesh, but before it could, Walt and Chris twisted the net tight. Chris handed the scoop to Walt and went into the shed. In a moment, he came back out, carrying a sickle they used to keep the weeds and grass down around the apron. With a *thwack* he cut the head off the snake.

Vivien felt sorry for the poor thing. It wasn't fair for it to be killed when it hadn't harmed anyone. Nor did she believe the serpent came there of its own will.

The day before, high winds rocked the trailers in the park, dirt devils swirled between the homes and around the empty areas. Trash cans were turned over, leaves and trash blew into the pool, and the soldiers worked all over the post to batten down even heavy equipment. The weatherman talked of gale force and hurricane force winds.

Is it possible for a ghost to control nature? Vivien asked herself.

The next night, a storm rolled in. Alarms sounded. The family raced away from the trailer in the car while the radio announcer described destruction from a tornado speeding through the darkness toward Camp Breckinridge. With his description, Daddy drove away from the path of destruction.

MANY OF THE RESIDENTS OF THE PARK DID THE SAME. THE MOODYS took shelter with their stored furniture like before. Again, Mr. Moody invited them to shelter there, but Daddy didn't think it any safer than the trailer.

Vivien scooted forward, resting her chin on the back of the front seat between Mama and Daddy. Debris reflected the headlights, blown about by the winds, swirling, other times appearing and disappearing so fast she could only see the motion.

A medium-sized tree branch hit the top of the car and bounced to the pavement on the other side. Headlights from behind shone from the car of another family racing to safety.

Suddenly, a woman's figure glowed in the headlights. Daddy hit the brakes and swerved to the right onto the shoulder of the road. Vivien blinked and the woman disappeared.

"What the hell?" Daddy said.

"I don't know," Mama said, looking from one side of the road to the other.

They didn't feel a bump, as if they'd hit something. The Chevy sped up.

Vivien bit her lip and leaned back in the seat. She'd recognized the woman. Nurse Armstrong.

At last, the weatherman announced the storm had moved on and the rest of the night would be calm. Daddy pulled the car into a farm lane and turned off the engine. The only light came from the radio. Lauren lay sleeping on her side of the back seat, unaware of the good news. Mama and Daddy spoke in low tones, thinking both girls slept.

Vivien lay opposite Lauren. She felt responsible. Nurse Armstrong insisted she was her daughter no matter what Vivien said. But the newspaper article she'd found proved the baby died. Could the ghost be convinced her baby didn't survive, so Vivien couldn't be her?

She could go back to the newspaper office and tear the story out of the archive copy, but it went against her principles. It might be the only copy in the whole world and tearing it out would be criminal. Her experience with libraries made her very aware of the value of printed material.

The clock on the yellow range read 1:27 when they got home. Mama carried Lauren to her bed and tucked her in. Daddy carried Vivien, who had finally dozed off. She woke as he laid her down. Mama helped them both get into their pajamas. The danger — and the day — had passed.

SHE WOKE TO THE SOUND OF A TRAIN IN THE DISTANCE. AS SHE listened in the dark, the sound grew closer, louder. Suddenly she remembered: there were no train tracks near them. Mama said tornados sounded like freight trains.

She jumped from bed and ran into her parents' room.

"Mama! Mama! It's a tornado."

Daddy spoke first. "What is it? What's wrong?"

Light from the pole outside shone through the curtain. He rubbed his eyes, trying to get rid of the sleepiness. He slurred his words from sleep and being wakened so suddenly.

Mama said, "What's wrong?"

"Daddy! It's a tornado. Don't you hear it? Mama said they sound like freight trains."

They said nothing for the space of several heartbeats. "Glenn?" Mama said.

"Vivien thinks she hears a tornado."

Why didn't they get up? They had to get away! The sound of the train grew louder and louder.

"I don't hear anything," Mama said.

"Me neither," Daddy said. "Vivien . . ."

She realized the sound faded as if the train — or tornado — moved on. Tears stung her eyes.

"Daddy . . ."

"It's alright, Viv," he said. "Just a bad dream."

He swung his legs over the side of the bed and sat up. His arms wrapped around her, pulling her close. He seldom showed much affection and she stiffened.

"A nightmare," he said.

The stubble of his beard pressed against her cheek and she leaned against him, putting her chin on his shoulder. He smelled of tobacco and Old Spice after shave. Mama brushed her arm where it wrapped around Daddy's neck. At last, she felt safe.

"You're all right," Mama said.

After another moment, Daddy pulled away. "All better?" he asked. She nodded. "Let's get you back in bed, then."

She turned toward the hall and he put his hand on her shoulder, guiding her. When he lifted the sheet on the bed, she crawled in. He leaned down and kissed her forehead. "Night."

"Night," she said.

He left and a moment later she heard the bed squeak in the back bedroom as he climbed in. Mama and Daddy whispered for a little while, then his snoring filled the silence.

She listened in the darkness. The sound of an approaching train came to her again, this time a memory. When she was seven, they lived in Colorado Springs, and Mama often sent her to a neighborhood grocer to pick up a few things. To get there, she had to cross a railroad track.

She'd gone there many times, often when a train passed through. She stood close to the tracks, feeling the vibrations, and the wind raised by its passing. Then, one day, the sound and sight of the train coming nearer, filled her with terror. For an instant, she stayed rooted to the spot. Abruptly, she turned and ran away.

She ran fast, blindly, her heart beating fast, just like tonight. Nearly a block away, she looked back. The caboose passed and the train rumbled out of sight. The sound faded. She sat down on a bench outside of the flower shop, breathing hard, hands clenched into fists.

When she finally got home, Mama asked what took so long. "I had to wait for a train," she said simply, unable to explain her sudden panic.

From then on, every time she encountered a train, she ran, putting as much distance between herself and the tracks as she could. Once the train passed, she could go on.

They'd moved yet again and there were no train tracks to walk across. Until tonight, she had not felt that fear again.

The memory ended, but not the fear. A young woman shouldn't be scared by such things, she scolded herself. She threw off the sheet and turned over, fell asleep, and dreamed of trains and tornados rushing by.

SEVENTEEN

"The top of the car isn't damaged much." Daddy and Mama sat at the table when the girls entered the trailer. Daddy had taken the Chevy into the shop in the morning to see how much it would cost to get the top fixed where the tree branch landed, and then to the insurance office to see if they would pay it. They wouldn't. So, Daddy justified not getting it fixed. Vivien was disappointed as the dent in the top made the car look trashy. Daddy mostly cared if the car ran well, and he was a good mechanic. It was six years old but he hoped to get another couple of years out of it.

Their bathing suits had dried while they walked from the pool. The afternoon heat already made them want to get back in the water.

"Your nose looks bad," Mama said.

Vivien reached up to touch the scabs on her nose from sunburn. She'd forgotten her straw hat again.

"You'll have permanent freckles there."

After her punishment lifted, both girls spent most of the day at the pool, now. Vivien still hung around Walt as much as she could, but her feelings became sadder than before. She would always be a little girl to him. Soon, they would move away and he would forget all about her. At least, with his help, she could now swim better.

Mama and Daddy returned to their conversation as the two girls enjoyed Mama's Waldorf salad, with the usual sweet iced tea.

After lunch, they had to hang around home for at least an hour before they could go back in the pool. Per and Karl didn't come back outside. Their mother probably kept them in to do their chores, while they waited for the hour to pass.

The past two days had been quiet. Between the pool opening and not having another period, she enjoyed her days much more. Mama warned her she might have her next one soon and she would have to keep an eye on things. Or it might not happen again for a few months.

She'd stayed away from the hospital in hopes that the ghost would leave her alone. But her appearance during the storm, and luring Lauren to the pool during the night, meant she wasn't trapped in the derelict building.

Vivien still wanted to find out more about Nurse Armstrong and Hans, but wasn't sure where to get more information. Was the baby girl named? She knew some people gave babies names even if they didn't live long.

One of Mama's friends at Ft. Knox had a baby boy who died right after birth. Mama said they were Catholic, and they named him before burying him. Everyone acted so sad, but she'd heard Mama whispering to a friend the baby had been deformed, and probably wouldn't have lived long.

She planned to go back to the hospital when she went for a walk that evening and try to tell Nurse Armstrong what she'd found out in the library and newspaper office. As much as she wanted to go, she also was afraid. Would the truth make the ghost angry or sad? Would she leave once she knew her baby died?

Mama said losing a child hurt more than any other loss. Vivien wondered at the time if fathers suffered as much.

Daddy rarely showed sympathy or any feelings, really, except when he got mad. She saw Mama accept those moments when he should be sympathetic and Vivien guessed she accepted it too. Men couldn't help being that way.

The four of them got to the pool by mid-afternoon and stayed until time for supper. Vivien spent much of the time worrying about whether she should visit the hospital to tell Lucille what she'd found out. She decided to go, whether for her benefit or the ghost's she couldn't say for sure.

She managed to slip away after supper, leaving Lauren to play with the boys when they came over. They almost always got together every evening to play hide and seek or tell ghost stories. It hit her, how much she would miss them when summer ended and her family moved away.

Daddy still didn't know for sure where they would go. He said it might be France, which would be okay. She'd checked out more books from the library on both France and Japan. Japan appealed to her more, in part because of Mrs. Warner's stories and souvenirs, but France had an interesting history.

She stopped daydreaming when she reached the hospital entrance. The buildings had been empty for several years, yet in some ways they looked fresh and nearly new. They never saw a broken window, and the paint didn't peel very much, still protecting the wooden siding. A temporary building thumbing its nose at the elements.

Living in the south for years accustomed anyone to the look of decay and age in buildings. Why didn't these fall apart like others?

She took a deep breath and climbed the steps. Time to confront Nurse Armstrong.

She used a stone to prop open the outer door. The building creaked more than usual as she walked through the corridor toward the empty room. She shivered and began to regret coming.

She opened the inner door, into the room where the ghost appeared. Hesitant to go inside, she stood next to the doorway. A baby's cry came out of the twilight in the room. Vivien rushed in and saw a bundle lying on the floor. It was wrapped in a blanket and, when she picked it up, it felt lighter than she expected. Cold air wafted up to her face when she folded back the corner of the blanket to see its face. "Oh!" She nearly dropped the small bundle.

Milky eyes flashed from the face, the skin wrinkled and grey. She wanted to put it back down but uncovered it instead. A baby girl, naked under the blanket. Its tiny body covered with skin as grey as the face. She kept crying yet lay perfectly still in Vivien's arms.

"What is that?" Nurse Armstrong's voice demanded.

"I think it's your baby. Your little girl? Don't you want to see her?" With shaking hands, Vivien held out the small bundle. *Please take it.*

Nurse Armstrong came closer and looked down at the baby. "It's not my daughter." She stepped back and held out a hand to Vivien. "You are my daughter."

Vivien lay the baby at the ghost's feet and backed away. The baby wailed. Lucille picked it up and cradled it. "What's wrong with it?"

"She's dead, like you."

"No! You're trying to fool me."

She threw the baby to the floor. It screamed. Nurse Armstrong's rage beat against Vivien in waves. The building shook, bounced up and down, throwing her to the floor. Stunned, Vivien lay still, waiting for the building to stop moving. She closed her eyes. Why had she ever come back here?

The sound and shaking of the building stopped. Vivien put her head down on her arm. She lay there on the floor, trying to stop trembling. When she raised her head and opened her eyes, she saw nothing but darkness.

She whimpered and stumbled toward the wall, hands outstretched. The floor felt solid under her feet. The wall solid against her hand when she reached it.

Silence wrapped around her. She called out, but the sound of her voice muffled. Suddenly, something growled to her right, low enough to make her think she imagined it. When she looked toward the doorway, she thought she saw movement. The smell of dirt and grass and long dead vegetation filled her nostrils.

Dizziness overwhelmed her and she pressed shaking hands against the wall. She wanted to run, but her legs barely held her upright. The same as at the railroad tracks. She lowered herself to the floor.

If only Mama would open the door and turn on the light. But she hadn't come with her, didn't know Vivien was in danger.

A large body moved with a rustling noise. Imagination conjured up a huge snake, a tiger, maybe . . .

Vivien wrapped her arms around herself and rested her forehead on her knees, drawn up toward her chest. Part of her wanted to see what roamed in the darkness. Part of her feared to look. Another low growl made her raise her head. She'd been stupid to come. She wanted to go home.

Another low growl.

"Where are you?" she cried out. *Please. Someone answer.*

"I'm not your daughter," she yelled. "Your daughter died. You saw her." She strained to see and the lighter grey of the windows slowly came into view. "She died the same time you did."

A long sigh filled the air, making her think of a giant saddened by her words. Something rustled off to one side. Nothing visible.

"Would you treat your own daughter this way? Scaring her half to death?"

She strained to hear anything. She listened so hard, her ears rang.

"Where are you?"

Tears gathered in her eyes and she angrily brushed them away with her fingertips. *I'm not a little girl anymore.*

"I'm here," the familiar voice said at last.

EIGHTEEN

Vivien looked toward the far corner. Lucille stood there, white in a sea of black.

"This —" she motioned with her hand indicating the darkness, "—— is where I have slept all these years. This sham. This monstrosity of a world."

"You said you were asleep."

"A kind of sleep. Nightmare, really. I didn't know who I was, where I was, why I was here. Nothing. It's a punishment."

"For what?"

The ghost looked at her for a long moment. Vivien swallowed hard, afraid to ask the one question which frightened her more. "Am I dead?"

Lucille laughed, ridiculing the question. "No. I wouldn't kill you. Unless it's the only way I can keep you with me."

"I'm not your daughter."

"You keep saying that." Lucille stomped her foot and her eyes narrowed. "You are my daughter."

"I *have* a mother and —"

"Enough. You haven't learned anything. I am your

mother."

"I wish I could show you —"

"Whatever you've been told or read is all lies. Everyone hated me. They would say anything."

"Would they put on Hans's grave marker that he had a family in Germany?"

"They died. He told me they were killed in a British airstrike."

That pulled her up short. It might be true. It might also be true other people in their world hated them. What she had seen in the memory when the other nurse held the baby — her anger —made it seem likely everyone lied about him and Lucille. And if the townspeople did kill Hans . . .

She'd seen such hatred once before. When they lived in Tennessee, a group of young white boys attacked a black boy. They cut his lip and bruised his cheek. She'd stood several feet away, frozen in place by the brutality. The white boys walked away, one of them laughing. The black boy sat on the ground and she saw anger in his expression, which faded to resignation. Resignation, or lack of hope?

She felt the same way herself, now. How could she hope to get home, back to her family? In her mind's eye, she saw Lauren splashing in the pool. Walt stood watching her and the other kids. She wanted to be older. She wanted to be old enough for Walt to look at her the way he looked at the older girl. Old enough to always save her little sister.

Lucille looked satisfied when Vivien glanced up.

The ghost could bring Lauren here, like she led her to the pool. She could take her life away from her. How long could either of them survive? Since she got here, she'd been neither hungry nor thirsty. Could she stay here for years?

"I can and I will. You or your sister. Your family. I can bring you all into my hell."

"What do you want? It can't just be me."

"I want you to waken Hans, as you did me. I want us to be a family."

"What?" She nearly shouted. "I have no idea how I woke you up, or even if I did. I can't wake him up. I've already been to his grave. There's nothing there but a marker."

"You're his daughter, too. You must be able to waken him."

"But I'm not. I don't know why you woke up or came back or whatever you did. But I didn't do it." Her voice broke and her body shook as she sobbed.

"You came to where I died."

"Yes, but —"

"Go home. Find a way. Or else your sister . . ."

She turned and walked away, fading until nothing remained.

Vivien put her hands over her face again, then wiped at the tears with her fingertips. She couldn't let Lauren be taken by Lucille. How could she convince her parents the ghost existed? That they needed to protect themselves from a ghost?

She wiped away the tears with the hem of her shirt. Dim light replaced darkness. She sat on the red linoleum floor of the hospital.

Her knees shook so hard she couldn't stand. Her mind screamed for her to get up, get home. But her legs wouldn't move when she tried. Her hands, resting in her lap, trembled. At last, she grabbed one hand with the other, squeezed, and the shaking slowed, then stopped.

First, she got to all fours, waiting for her body to calm. Slowly, she pushed herself to her feet, taking deep breaths. She'd never felt so lost. She wanted to run outside but her legs felt too weak. The air in the room grew warmer.

She wanted to forget. Convince herself it never happened, except in her imagination.

NINETEEN

"I'm sorry I didn't get back sooner."

Mama looked up from her crocheting and smiled. "It hasn't been very long. You just lost track of time."

Vivien looked at the clock on the stove. Not quite seven o'clock in the evening. The same day? She realized she'd been gone less than two hours. It felt like a whole day.

All the way home, she'd tried to think of a way to tell Mama what happened, to convince her it was real. But the closer she got, the more the memory became fuzzy. The details faded, but the fear did not.

What should she do to protect her family? Would telling them — whether they believed her or not — be a good idea?

Daddy would want to take her back to the doctor. The doctor would agree it was — what did they call it in one of the books she read? Female hysteria. It was what men called it when they couldn't cope with a woman's emotions, Mama said.

She wished there was someone to talk to. Someone closer to her own age and with whom she could compare thoughts and emotions. Lauren was too young. Per and Karl? No, they were boys and wouldn't understand what it was like to be a girl. What it was like to see an angry ghost.

Certain of what she saw, she feared for her family. She must protect them.

Hans.

More than anything, she felt certain she shouldn't waken another ghost. She had no idea how she woke up Lucille, or even if she did. What she needed to do was put her back to sleep. But maybe if she could waken Hans, he could get Lucille to understand her own baby died.

Next morning, started as every day did, except the Warners had left before sunrise to visit family in Maryland, so she wasn't heard calling "Chisei," her little dog. The name meant "intelligence" in Japanese. Vivien sat on the picnic table, still worrying what to do. Soon Lauren would come outside and the two of them would go to the pool where they would play until noon. Then home for lunch, wait an hour, back to the pool, and so on.

More people moved into the trailer park every day. "Summer soldiers" and their families arriving in waves each week for a two-week annual training. More people in the pool, more kids shouting and screaming, never there long enough to get to know them.

She sat on the edge of the pool, near the shallow end, dangling her feet in the water. The breathlessly hot day and the activity around her distracted her from her troubles. She didn't see the little boy at first. The toddler had been sitting in the shallow end, splashing the water with his hands. His mother sat nearby, her feet dangling in the water, talking and laughing with another woman.

One moment the boy splashed water with great joy. The next he lay face down in the water, utterly still.

Vivien shouted and jumped in. She reached the child quickly and snatched him up. From behind her, his mother screamed. As Vivien turned him over, she saw Lucille's face. The ghost faded, and the boy's face replaced hers. His eyes opened wide, his mouth gasped for air. The mother snatched him away without a thank you. "Bobby," she cried.

"Good job," Walt said. He had jumped in right behind her but she hadn't been aware of him.

"What?" She had barely registered that he stood so close.

"You saved him. The kid doesn't know that, and she's too frightened. But I will remember, and so will you."

Walt will remember, she thought and believed it was enough.

When she told Mama before lunch, she congratulated her. "Did his mama thank you?"

"No."

"It's all right. She was probably shaken by what happened."

"I know." After the adrenalin rush, she'd had time to remember Lucille's face in place of the child's.

After Daddy left for HQ, and they'd finished cleaning up, Mama decided she would go over the girls' reading material with them. Every so often, she looked through the books they had, and listed what they had read.

Mama had graduated from high school, but her family didn't have the money for her or her three sisters to get any further education. They graduated from high school, got married, and had children, making any further education a waste in their parents' eyes. Still, she belonged to the Book-of-the-Month club and read a lot herself, both fiction and nonfiction. With her fascination with movies, she sometimes read biographies of movie stars. She never told her girls what they could or could not read, but preferred they read good books, not trashy ones.

Mama worked in a café where she met Daddy when he was posted to Camp Forrest, another temporary training camp outside Manchester where she had lived her whole life. She fell in love with the young soldier and got married. "He was so handsome in his uniform," she always said. It seemed so romantic to Vivien.

"The two boys never came back home," she had said of her brothers. "Owen, the eldest brother, served in World War II and returned unscathed. He went to a trade school in New Mexico, and worked on some sort of top-secret project, afterward. When the Korean War began, Benjamin, the youngest, went into the Air Force. He went to college under the G.I. Bill. Lucille, Mama's closest sister, went to business school and had a job as a secretary at the high school."

"Lucille," Vivien whispered. She glanced toward Mama to see if she'd heard. She'd not realized Mama's closest sister had the same name as the ghost.

The hour passed and the two girls walked back to the pool. Fewer people came in the heat of the afternoon. Some of the women with small children would be putting them down for their naps. Those with slightly older children likely had work to do at home. Many of them would return after supper. For now, though, a few older children and the lifeguards had the pool to themselves.

Vivien jumped in where the water was just over her head. She kicked off the bottom and rose to the surface. After a couple of laps across the pool, she got out. Per and Karl were in the water horsing around.

"Hey, Per!" He waved. "Keep an eye on Lauren for me? A few minutes." She motioned toward Lauren playing with another girl her age. She wrapped the towel around her waist and tucked in the end.

"Sure," Per said. He splashed his brother one more time and climbed out to sit on the concrete apron. Karl paddled over to the two girls.

"I'll be back in a minute," Vivien said.

She watched only a few seconds to be sure Walt's attention focused on the same girl from the night Lauren almost drowned. Chris, the other lifeguard, disappeared into the shed.

Vivien walked around the pool and slipped into the woods. Again, the coolness made her shiver. The sound of voices from the pool faded. She went straight to the cemetery and crouched on her heels at Hans' grave.

Should she call out to him? Tell him what happened? He needed to convince Lucille their daughter had died, like them. Maybe they could all be together again. Could they? The preacher at Grandma's church had said we join our loved ones in heaven when we die, but this was different. Lucille hadn't left. What about Hans and the baby?

She sat on her heels and reached out to touch the metal marker. The iron felt ice-cold against her fingertips and she shivered. The light around her faded. Already shaded by the woods, it grew darker. She stood in the twilight and peered at the black forms of trees and bushes. She hadn't noticed the birds until they stopped singing. Unsettled by the silence, she turned and hurried back into the sunshine.

TWENTY

Daddy didn't speak all during dinner. In spite of her own distraction, Vivien noticed, and wondered why. They enjoyed very little conversation at the table on any night, but tonight there was less than usual, in spite of Mama's attempts to draw them out.

Vivien and Lauren cleared the table and started doing the dishes. Vivien washed and Lauren dried. They usually bickered the whole time, but tonight they were silent. Daddy remained at the table, finishing his iced tea. His mood hovered over them and they worked quietly.

"I think we might not be going to Japan in August," he said, suddenly. He tipped up the glass and drank the last of his iced tea.

"Where, then?" Mama asked.

"Looks like it'll be France."

The two of them began discussing the possible new posting.

"Did you hear that?" Lauren whispered.

Vivien's heart sank. She'd learned quite a bit about both

countries, and believed she was reconciled to accept either one. But Mrs. Warner's stories of their two years there, and all of the beautiful things she brought back, had made her want to go to Japan more than anything. She'd come to expect it.

Why France of all places? The country was known for wine, and chateaux, fashion and perfume.

She tried to come to terms with the news with thoughts of leaving Camp Breckinridge as the good news. Once they left, she wouldn't have to worry about Lucille anymore.

". . . you and the girls won't be able to come. Not for a year, probably."

"Why?" Vivien's ears pricked up. Why wouldn't they be able to go with him? If they didn't go, where would they live?

Daddy explained the Army wouldn't pay for the family to go until after his next promotion in a year or less.

"Where will we go?" Mama asked. "I guess we can live at Mama's."

They went on discussing the possibility of moving to Grandma's. If she agreed, they could park their trailer beside the old house. Water and electricity would be a bit of a problem, but Daddy would figure it out.

Vivien loved her grandma very much, but she knew she could be cantankerous, the word Daddy had used once to describe his mother-in-law. She lived in the country in a house that was part log cabin. The house didn't have running water; only a well where they drew water with a wooden bucket. An outhouse stood next to the garden, which both girls hated. It stank, the corners were cobwebbed, and Lauren once found a snake hanging from the rafters.

They'd both helped her in the garden a couple of times when they visited one summer. Bugging potatoes wasn't a favorite occupation of either of them, but overall, they enjoyed living in the country in summer. They had no idea what Middle Tennessee might be like in the winter.

All possible problems with moving disappeared in her delight at knowing the ghost would stay behind. She need not worry about waking up Hans or putting Lucille back to sleep.

An hour after lunch, the sisters met up with their friends, and they walked toward the pool together. The girls were dying to tell them where they would be going. They mentioned the year in Tennessee only in passing.

"I thought you wanted to go to Japan," Per said. "You read all those books." They walked side-by-side while their siblings walked behind them.

"I hoped it would be but turns out it will probably be France. I don't know anyone who's been there."

"My dad was there during the war," Per said.

"Well, yeah," Vivien said. "Daddy, too. But it's different now."

"How different?"

"I don't know. Except there's no war."

Per shrugged. "We'll miss you."

She felt the same way, but his saying it out loud surprised Vivien. Living in a more exotic place had begun to excite her. The people spoke French, of course, and she didn't know a word of it, except "oui" which she'd learned from a Tom and Jerry comic book. She wished they could go with Daddy right away. The year in Tennessee paled in comparison to the thrill of living in a foreign country.

Besides, nothing had been decided for certain. Except they would be moving somewhere before the end of August. The Moodys would be moving in about a year, too. Could the two families end up in the same place?

107

Crickets chirped and katydids buzzed from the distant trees. The quarter moon hovered high in the sky. A citronella candle flickered in an aluminum foil chicken-pot-pie pan sitting on the picnic table. Lights shone in windows of trailers, large and small, up and down the street, fewer to the right than to the left. A baby cried in the distance, turning to laughter the next minute. Other children's voices could be heard, but not the words. One trailer had a window-mounted water cooler, the motor whirring in the soft evening air. Grown-ups' voices wafted on the slight breeze coming from the direction of the pool.

Mama and Mrs. Moody sat in the metal lawn chairs, talking married women talk. Daddy and Mr. Moody sat at one end of the picnic table, probably swapping war stories. The four kids sat at the other end of the table, Per standing at the end, the others sitting on the benches.

They were bored, having already played hide and seek. Karl wanted to tell ghost stories, but the girls voted him down. Fireflies had disappeared by this time in summer. Mama said the humidity had dropped and the temperatures would soon be cooling too much for them. They tried to play cards, but they couldn't read the cards in the low light.

Mostly, being in the pool much of the day had tired them out, along with chasing each other in the spaces between the trailers afterward in a game of tag. If only the Warners hadn't left, they might tell them stories of the places they'd been posted. Maybe they'd lived in France? Mrs. Warner never said, but Vivien would bet she hadn't heard half of their adventures.

Vivien sat with her back against the table, her skinny legs stretched out. Still skinny, not curvy. The adults' voices murmured, the insects buzzed and chirped. The warm night air caressed her skin. Next thing she knew, Mama patted her shoulder and told her, "Time for bed." Vivien stood, trying to shake off sleep, but it was a losing battle. The Moodys drifted toward their own trailer.

Vivien stumbled up the metal steps and pulled the screen door open. She washed up quickly. Daddy carried Lauren, already asleep, and put her to bed. Mama and Daddy went into the bedroom at the back and closed the accordion door. Vivien changed into the baby doll pajamas and lay down on the bed.

The new fan in the living room drew air through the window over her bed and across, cooling her slightly. August was usually one of the hottest months of the year, but the furnace-like heat of July had not yet given way. Evenings wouldn't cool until early September. At least that was how it went the first year they lived in Kentucky.

This summer had been odd, though. Like the number of thunderstorms they'd been having. The whole weather pattern had changed. She'd heard Daddy talking about it to Mr. Moody.

She wanted to sit up and fight off sleep so she could study these new facts logically. Or illogically if she admitted she thought Lucille might be responsible for the changes. But she drifted off, the sound of the fan lulling her to sleep.

She jerked awake. Something woke her. A sound, a movement in the darkness relieved only by the glow from the street-light. Short of breath, she crawled out of bed. Suddenly, she needed to know Lauren was safe.

Padding to her sister's bed, Vivien reached out and patted the bed with clammy hands. Empty. She listened for Daddy's snoring but a roaring in her ears blocked any sound. Slowly, she moved toward the back and pulled the accordion door aside. The yellow glow of the streetlight revealed her parents' empty bed.

Vivien ran to the front door and opened it. She pushed it to the right as far as it would go, felt it latch against the outer wall. A dog barked in the distance. She stepped down in her bare feet, onto a rough road instead of the patio. It stretched right and left, dimly lit by more streetlights spaced very far apart. Random piles of debris partially blocked it. Piles of rubble lay everywhere. Phone wires hung from poles.

Children appeared from her right, moving silently, their clothes dirty and ragged. They scanned the rubble, climbing piles of it here and there, searching through the debris. Most of what they picked up they discarded. Occasionally, one would put a small bit in a coat or pants pocket.

Vivien stayed as still as she could, hoping they didn't see her.

A skinny dog approached, its head held low, tail between its legs. One of the boys picked up a rock or piece of brick and threw it at the animal. It whined and crouched, the missile landing a few inches from it. The children went back to scrounging and the dog slunk away.

A WARM BREEZE WAFTING THROUGH THE WINDOW FLUTTERED THE short curtains over the vanity. Vivien opened her eyes and listened in the darkness. Silence.

A dream. Simply a dream.

She'd gotten books out of the library over the weekend with pictures of France and they showed the country the year the war ended, the year of her birth. Some cities and towns were a bombed-out mess. She sighed and took deep breaths. The books and pictures must have made her dream about it.

A niggling doubt crept into her mind and she slid out of bed. Slipping into the hall, she passed her sister's bed where Lauren slept peacefully. As quietly as possible, she moved to the accordion door. She pulled the magnetic latch apart and pushed the door open a few inches. Daddy snored, lying beside Mama.

Finally, she went to the front door and opened it as quietly as she could. Still, the door and screen door, latched together, rattled, sounding loud in the silence. She listened but no one stirred.

Outside, all looked as it should be. Yet, Vivien felt uneasy. She'd never had a dream like it before. So clear, in both sight and sound. Had Lucille made her dream it somehow, to make her afraid? A threat maybe? If so, did it mean the ghost knew they were all leaving soon?

She shook her head. Just the pictures in the books.

Worse — if Lucille did know, would she try to stop them?

TWENTY-ONE

Could the silence in one place be bigger than the silence in another?

Vivien knew the silence inside the trailer at night. It felt close, comforting, punctuated by the ticking of the clock and whirring of the fan. Out in the open, the silence felt large, stretching into the next county. And it felt soft, thin, like the difference between a flannel sheet and a regular cotton sheet.

She stepped down from the picnic table and looked around. The darkness closed in. Lucille was coming.

She started to go inside. She would be safe in the trailer with her family. But what if Lucille followed? Then they would all be in danger. She couldn't lead the ghost to her family.

She decided she would lead Lucille away. She headed to the road and ran toward the pool. The cemetery. If she could get to the cemetery, maybe Hans would sense their presence and . . . What?

At least, Lucille could be made to see Hans's grave. She

suddenly wondered where Lucille's and the baby's graves might be. Until now, she hadn't thought of them.

Cold air blew against her back. She looked behind but saw nothing except the dark outlines of the trailers. Reaching the pool, she stopped, and the cold air surrounded her. Her baby doll pajamas were light, and goose bumps broke out on her arms.

It's the cool air. I'm not afraid.

Skirting the pool, she made her way into the woods. Without a light, she stumbled through brambles and tripped over vines. Her arms took the brunt of the fall as she held her hands up to protect her face.

The moment she entered the cemetery, the moon broke through the clouds, the light flowing through the trees and bushes. Vivien found Hans's marker by memory, though of course she couldn't read the inscription in the dark.

Now what should she do?

"Hans, wake up," she said.

A breeze raised more goose bumps and she turned looking for the ghostly figure in its nurse's uniform. She felt Lucille's presence. She had followed. Why didn't she appear?

"What is this place?" The voice came from somewhere back the way Vivien had come.

"It's the POW cemetery."

"Why did you come here?"

"Hans is buried here. Your Hans."

"Where?"

"Right here." Vivien pointed at the marker.

"Poor Hans. He never got to see our baby." Lucille materialized slowly, white smoke swirling into a woman's form.

"Maybe she's with him."

"No! You are my daughter."

"Our daughter is here." A man's heavily accented voice came from behind Vivien. "I have her safe."

"No. Our daughter lives. She's here."

"*Nein, Liebchen.* She is in my arms. Our baby."

A keening rose in volume, until Vivien thought her ear drums would burst. She pressed her palms over her ears trying to block it, but it penetrated her whole body until she thought she would burst. Then suddenly, it stopped.

Panting, Vivien reached out a hand to a tree to steady herself. Tears blinded her. A cold hand took hold of her arm and pulled her away. She stumbled. The grip of the hand kept her from falling.

"Look at her," Lucille's voice said.

Vivien didn't want to look at either of them. Curiosity made her look up, though, and she saw Hans. His clothes — uniform — looked dark grey. He wore no hat. Handsome in spite of being so white, Vivien could see why Lucille fell in love with him.

She recognized the blanket bundled in his arms. A small hand reached up toward the man's face. He looked down and smiled.

"Come closer, *Liebchen.* Look at our baby. She is so beautiful."

This had to be the same ghostly baby she found in the hospital. Lucille backed away, wanting nothing to do with it, then or now.

"Go back to sleep, Hans. You and that creature."

She jerked Vivien around and started away from the cemetery. Vivien tried to break free but the grip on her arm tightened. Vivien yelped in pain and fear of where Lucille might be taking her.

"You mustn't go back to the hospital," Hans yelled. "It is your prison."

Cold wrapped around Vivien, different from what she experienced earlier. It held her tightly. She realized Lucille had stopped, gripped by the same frigid air.

The nurse turned back toward Hans pulling Vivien with her. "You won't stop me."

A burst of glacial energy burst from her. It enveloped Vivien and spread toward Hans as an icy mist. He disappeared from view. The baby wailed. Vivien's teeth chattered. Her knees wobbled. Frost formed on her fingers, spread upward to her hand.

She pulled hard against Lucille's hold but couldn't break free. "Please," she sobbed, but Lucille ignored her. "If you love me, let me go. Please."

Lucille looked down at her. She released the arm and Vivien fell to the ground where she lay still, shivering, thinking she should feel the warmth of the ground beneath her.

The sound of breaking glass caught her attention. She raised up on one elbow. Not glass. Shards of ice, created by the opposing blasts of air, fell to the ground.

The battle stopped, but the baby continued to wail. Lucille quickly reached down to grab Vivien's arm, but something pushed her back. She crawled among the rotting vegetation, trying to put space between her and Lucille.

"You will come with me," Hans said. He held his hand straight out.

Lucille fought as some force pulled her toward the grave. Her cap came loose and fell to the ground, freeing her long, dark hair. She struggled harder when Hans turned her away from him, toward another marker. When she reached it, she looked back at him with a look of pure terror.

"Sleep now," Hans said.

Lucille writhed, but slowly, she disappeared into the ground. The ground rippled, then stilled. Hans looked over to

Vivien. He smiled and Vivien wondered if having both the woman he loved and their baby made him happy. Would they rest in each other's arms? He nodded, put both arms around the baby and sank away.

Vivien rolled onto her back. She lay there quietly for some time, listening to her own heartbeat. After several minutes, she crawled on all fours to the spot where Lucille disappeared. She felt for the iron marker and rocking it back and forth, pulled it from the ground. In a shaft of moonlight, she read the name on it: Lucille Armstrong, RN. She found no words on the back of it.

TWENTY-TWO

Vivien ran as fast as she could. The surface of the road shone in the moonlight. Tears blurred her vision. Close to home she saw . . .

The spot was empty. The trailer gone. The Chevy gone.

"Mama," she cried. She sniffed and wiped tears from her eyes with the heel of her hand. The Murphys across the street had left. The Joneses on the other side were gone, as were the Warners.

How long had Lucille kept her in the graveyard?

How long before her family gave up on ever seeing her again?

They were supposed to be going to Tennessee. She knew where to go, but not how to get there.

Her shoulders dropped and, head down, she walked to the old picnic table, climbed up on the top, her feet on the bench. She cried softly until she had no more tears, until she coughed and couldn't get her breath.

When she looked up again, the main hospital building

stood against the lightening sky. Dawn would come in an hour or so. Even in the dark, she sensed the danger had passed. Lucille was at peace, or at least Hans would keep her out of harm's way and keep her from harming others.

She was tired and sad, and sleep slipped up on her. Taking a deep breath, she lay down on the picnic tabletop and closed her eyes. Her body still trembled from the cold and fear.

"Vivien?"

She jerked awake, afraid Lucille had come back for her. Her heart raced. She raised her head to see the one person she longed for most coming toward her.

"Mama?"

Mama stood next to the table. Vivien jumped down and Mama wrapped her arms around her. Vivien knew she was home when she smelled the violet scent her mother wore. Both of them cried tears of relief as Mama stroked her hair.

"I was so afraid when I woke up and found you gone," Mama said.

"You left . . ."

When Vivien looked over her mother's shoulder, the trailer sat in its place, the car parked where it should be.

"It was all gone a moment ago. The trailer, the car, you."

"You don't think I would leave without you, do you? You must have been dreaming. We still have a couple weeks before we move out."

They sat down. Mama held her close, and she felt warm and safe. She knew if Lucille had kept her away so long, the family would have been forced to move away without her. Daddy's strongest loyalty would always be to the Army.

"Is . . . is everything all right?" Mama asked.

"I think so. Lucille is gone."

"Good. I hope she's at peace."

Vivien told her mother what happened in the cemetery. When she described Lucille's grip on her arm and how cold she got, Mama stiffened beside her. She said nothing, letting her daughter talk.

"Well," Mama said. "We'll leave here soon enough. Things will be better once we get to Tennessee."

The bedroom light came on in the back bedroom. Daddy headed for the bathroom. Mother and daughter held hands as they walked to the door. Vivien went to her own bed and soon slept.

She woke up late that morning. Another hot day, and no one wanted to do much of anything. Per mentioned going to the hospital, but Vivien said they could all go exploring without her. She didn't think she would ever go there again. Besides, she wanted to enjoy the pool as long as possible since there wouldn't be one at Grandma's.

Mr. Moody and Daddy came home for lunch.

"I should know for sure where we're going this afternoon or tomorrow," Daddy said. "I'll get official orders next week."

Mama asked him where he thought they'd end up.

He turned to Vivien. "I know you'll be disappointed it isn't Japan, but France is a beautiful country."

"What was it like when you were there before?" she asked.

"The war was ending. The country had been pretty torn up. Probably a lot of things are different. The Frogs don't like Americans much right now."

"Frogs?"

"French people. They loved us when we liberated their country."

"They like wine there, don't they?"

"Yep, lots of it."

"I don't like wine," Lauren piped up.

"You've never had any," Vivien reminded her.

"No, but I don't like it."

Mama and Daddy smiled at each other and he got up to go back to work. After the required hour, the four trooped back to the pool. Vivien couldn't look at the woods behind it.

CHAPTER
TWENTY-THREE

The day before they left, Vivien went to the pool to say goodbye to Walt. Boxes sat on the floor of the trailer and soon the four of them would be in the car, driving down to Grandma's place.

Walt had already gone. Chris said he'd left for Ft. Campbell.

"He didn't even say goodbye," she muttered, her shoulders dropping.

"He left this for you." Chris held out a small paper bag.

Vivien opened it. He'd left her a small book of poetry by Emily Dickensen.

"He said some of the poems reminded him of you."

"Thank you." She clutched the book to her chest. She took a handkerchief out of her pocket and wiped away tears and blew her nose. No matter how many times they had to do it, she really hated leaving places.

In the evening, Daddy hooked the trailer up to the Chevy. Everyone gathered at their picnic table in the twilight. The men drank Falstaff beer, and the women and kids drank iced tea. She wished for fireflies one last time. A mockingbird called in the distance. A single mosquito buzzed around, everyone having a turn at swatting it away.

The sun went down and the air grew slightly cooler. Indian summer with fall on its way. Daddy would soon be on his way overseas, while the rest of the family settled in next to Grandma's old house, outside Manchester.

Vivien couldn't remember a minute of living there, although Mama said they had. They'd visited a couple of times, but only in the summer. This time, they would find out about fall, winter, and spring in Middle Tennessee.

Not something to be excited about, maybe. But she was an Army brat. And Army brats learned to live wherever the Army sent them.

ACKNOWLEDGMENTS

My wholehearted thanks go to librarians everywhere, especially those who answered the questions I could not have answered any other way.

And to members of the Dorsal Fin Society who helped to describe the almost indescribable. Also to Tom Howard and Paul Marek who critiqued every word. Also, to my editors, Alicia Dean and Savannah Thorne, whose eyes caught so much.

About the Author

Cary Herwig is an emerging author of middle grade/young adult horror fiction. This is the first in *The Army Brat Hauntings* series. This is Cary's twelfth published book.

You can find Cary's blog at https://caryosbornewriter. blogspot.com/ and email her at iroshiok@gmail.com.